Mercy of the Vampire King

A STEAMY VAMPIRE ROMANCE

THE VAMPIRE KINGS SERIES
BOOK ONE

RHIANNON FUTCH

Contents

One

The Blessing Story of the Twelve, as told by Conrí, father of Valdís

*　*　*

Once, in a time before people counted time in minutes and hours, days and years, twelve brave men existed. They had sent a grim beast to kill all the tribes by the others from across the oceans. It was a creature of many arms and razor-sharp teeth; a breath from it could melt a person where they stood. We had been an open country back then, but the jealousy of the ones we call other made us wary. We were advanced even then, and they coveted our advances. But the others had gods as jealous as they. They coveted our goddess's people and wanted us to convert or be destroyed. Their covetous god called the beast up from the depths and sent it racing for our shores.

Our people were terrified, and rightly so, for who would protect us from this fearsome beast?

The tribes gathered in the center of the continent, right about where the castle is now. The elders cried out to the goddess, is there no one to save us? That is when the twelve stepped forward. Each one volunteering to give his life that the rest might have a chance to live. They were young and in the prime of their adulthood, with everything to live for, yet they were willing to give it all up just to give the tribes a chance at surviving. Our Goddess blessed them, gave them a gift to help them be strong. This gift gave them greater strength, speed, and made them very hard to kill.

They met the hulking beast at the shore, and the fight lasted for days. The tribes could hear the beast roar when one of the twelve scored a blow. On the seventh day, the beast let out a wrenching cry and thunder shook the land.

The tribes watched for the return of the twelve all day. When no one appeared, they sent men to the shore to find them. They found the beast dead on the shore, and they saw the tracks where the men had fought the beast to death. But there were no tracks leading away from the beast. They cut the beast open, in case the men had been swallowed whole. Nothing.

Running back to the tribes, they were fast, like small children seeking their mother. They told the story of what they had seen and as they finished, the twelve appeared. Standing in the circle, a golden light surrounding them and the voice of the Goddess saying, "These men have saved us all, for what is a Goddess without her people? They are now the protectors and kings of this land. I have blessed them. They and those they choose will be here always to protect this land of mine and my people."

From that day forward, we have had the Twelve Kings protecting us from the ones across the ocean.

Two

Valdís

* * *

"It has to be now. Father has been dead near two weeks and she has put off the reading of the will four times already. You know as well as I do exactly what that means."

Dagma's head swivels again, watching to make sure no one comes close enough to hear our whispered conversation before she says, "I know. I know. But you have rarely been outside the castle and never by yourself. What if you get lost? What if someone attacks you? We could find you laying in a ditch and then she's got what she wants, doesn't she?"

"I'll be careful. And I have been outside the castle by myself. I just didn't tell anyone because I was sneaking out. I'll be okay, Dagma. It's probably safer for me out there than it is in here. Promise me, if I don't come back in time to not be missed, promise me you all will leave. Just walk away from this place. When I gain control, I will find you and rehire you at twice the pay. But I don't want you hurt, or worse, because she knows you are loyal to me."

Dagma sighs as her shoulders drop. "We will. But you better make it back. Or at least stay safe. We can get other jobs. Goddess knows they are plenty looking for help. All right, go. You have money with you? Hidden?"

"Yes, in all the secret spaces you installed in my clothing. I have to go. They will come back this way on patrol in ten minutes, and I need to be well out of sight when they get here." I throw my arms around her and hug her tightly, "I love you Dagma, stay safe till I can return old friend."

She gasps indignantly at the old part and I let go of her, rushing out the door and down the walk. The night is deeply dark, streetlights few and far between. Stopping at the side gate, I listen, just in case they walked faster this time. Hearing nothing, I swing the gate open, sending thanks to the Goddess that I thought to oil the hinges this morning. Closing it behind me, I face the night before I run down the street for some deeper shadows.

My father's oldest friend's residence is only two miles from our home. Happily, my eyes are better in the dark than during the day. I have never been overly fond of bright lights, and the night has always felt warmer, more welcoming. It is possible that I feel that way because my mother, Eirene, has always loved bright lights. She insisted the manor be brightly lit at all times, which is why the battery house has grown so large over the years.

Footsteps echo down the street and I panic that it's my

mother's guards. Looking around, I find a convenient alley and slip into the deeper darkness, a small alcove offering more cover than I had hoped to have. Letting my hair hang forward to further shadow my face, I watch the street as the footsteps come closer. My breath catches in my throat, the steps echo in my ears as they walk past my hiding space. I relax as the steps recede into the night.

Stepping quietly out of my hiding spot, I fly down the streets toward Ingemar's home. He just has to help me.

Ingemar's gates have never been such a welcome sight as they are tonight. The guard lets me in, though he has a half dozen questions about what I am doing out so late, unescorted. Pfft! As if I am not a full seventy years old! Just because our people are long lived does not make the seventy years I have been here dealing with the way my mother hates me worthless. It definitely does not mean I am as reckless as a twenty-year-old. What is up with everyone? Wait. I have made it a point to let everyone believe I stayed holed up in our estate, never venturing out without a guard or my father. I suppose I can't blame them, even if I really dislike all the stupid questions it is causing now.

Finally, at the front door, I knock and a servant quickly answers, admitting me to the drawing room. Ingemar is there not long after, I am so glad to see him. "Valdís, what are you doing here so late? Your mother must be worried sick about you, especially after losing your father so recently."

"She doesn't know I have left. She would have tried to

stop me from seeking your help if she knew. My mother is not who she seems. She is determined to wrest my inheritance from me and I deeply fear how the servants and workers would fare if she took control. The lands and people my father has tended so lovingly will go to ruin with her at the helm. She isn't the person everyone believes her to be. Will you help me?"

"I know your mother can be brash, but I am certain this is all just a misunderstanding. Now what exactly has she done? Do you have any evidence that she is attempting to take away your inheritance? And why is it going to you? That is a little odd. Usually it would go to the widow and then the children on her passing."

Sighing, I tell him, "I know. My father changed his will ten years ago. He wouldn't tell anyone why. It was right after he had recovered from that strange illness the doctors couldn't find a reason for. He got well and sent for his lawyers. Then he closeted himself in with them for hours before calling all of us in. Told us he was changing his will and I would be the inheritor of the estate. When I asked him why, all he would say was that my mother knew why. She destroyed some of his things while she screamed at him. She never said exactly why, but considering the things she has done to me, I think it is likely that she had tried to kill him. As for the inheritance, she has been continually rescheduling it. I feel certain she will do whatever is necessary to keep me from getting control of the estates."

He steeples his fingers in front of himself as he listens. His silence grates on my already frayed nerves. Finally, he sits up and calls for Hulthen. When he enters the room, he says, "Take Valdís to a room and begin preparations for a wedding." My gasp of outrage is loud, and he looks at me. "You will do much better once you have a husband to focus on. That will put an end to these delusions. You and Pelos have always gotten along so nicely. You will be fine companions in a marriage as well."

"Marriage?" I shriek, "You are out of your mind! I came to you for help! Not a forced marriage to your son!" His people grab my arms and start to drag me out of the room, "You were my father's best friend! How could you do this?"

He smiles, "Don't worry, I'll make sure you get your inheritance. You'll need it for my grandchildren."

"Grandchildren? Never! I will not!" His people shut the door behind us as I struggle to free myself. I fight them all the way to the second floor room they shove me into. The floor rushes up at me, it knocks the breath out of me and I lay there struggling to breathe as they slam the door behind me. Catching my breath, I push myself up and look around. The room is pleasant, and oh yes! It has a balcony. Think I'm unable to climb just because I'm a girl? Good. I love it when you underestimate me. The doors to the balcony aren't even locked. Stepping out, I look around. He doesn't appear to have anyone stationed out here. Excellent. The balcony has a regular, post type railing and a decent ledge to hang from. I lean out and see the big fucking columns. Great, probably not going to feel so hot sliding down that pole, but it should do the job. Climbing over the railing, I lower myself down and wrap my legs around the column, clenching my thighs around it as I lower myself to get my arms around it. I slide down it slowly and lower my feet to the ground instead of meeting it with more force. Feet on the ground, I take off for the wall. The wall is a little taller than my five foot nine frame, but with a jump at the wall, I am grasping the ledge and pulling myself up. Wriggling up onto the top ledge, I thank the Goddess I have been climbing over these types of walls for long enough to have the rhythm of it. Even if I don't have enough strength to be good at it.

Swinging my legs over the other side, I lower myself down and drop the last little bit to the ground. I think I heard a shout as I was going, but I can't be sure without waiting around to find out and I am surely not doing that.

Pelos

* * *

Father has somehow gotten Valdís here and says that we are getting married. I have had the hots for her since we were still in our twenties. That curvaceous body and olive skin paired with her dark hair. I have long wished for a convenient place to have her alone. And now, she is locked in one of our guest rooms until our wedding.

I am sure father won't mind if I sample the goods the night before the wedding. He said that he wanted her with child immediately. Almost like he invited me to start the process now. The room she is in is quiet. Perhaps she has gone to bed already. I let myself in with my key, making sure to lock the door behind me.

I look at the empty bed, and a bad feeling sweeps over me. A breeze touches my skin. I look at the balcony doors standing open to the night. Shit! Dashing across the room and stopping at the railing. I scan the yard and see a form dropping down over the wall. I call out, "Guards!" Turning, I run back to the bedroom door and let myself out. Running as fast as my feet will carry me to find my father, shouting the entire way for the guards.

My father is in his study and he is irate when he finds out they let her slip away. He sends five of his men out to bring her back, then he calls for his servant, "Hulthen!"

I watch as he enters the room, all stately and calm, as though he didn't run his ass over here like the hounds were after him. "Yes, sir? How can I help you?"

My father smiles, "I want you to visit the widow Eirene. Tell her that her daughter has been here telling stories about her that are obviously delusional, but even so, we would like to discuss a wedding between her and my Pelos. Pelos needs a wife to provide heirs. It isn't necessary that she is well acquainted with reality. Tell her we look forward to hearing from her. We have our people out right now, working to bring dear Valdís back here, where she will be safe with her soon to be husband."

My cock twitches at the thought of having Valdís here with me, but I keep my breath measured and even. Father will not tolerate any sort of tell toward my emotions. The only reason he did not beat me for the running is due to the fact that she must be brought back as soon as possible. Had I run in here so excited for no reason, it would not have gone well for me. Hulthen nods and retreats from the room, only turning when he is outside the door.

Father turns to me, "Where was she when you entered the room?"

"She was already climbing the wall. I realized the room was empty as soon as I turned from locking the door behind me. Getting to the open balcony with haste, I saw her dropping over the other side of the wall. I ran directly here after that."

He nods, "Very well. You have no responsibility in this and did as much as possible to mitigate the damage done by the servants that put her in the balcony room on the second floor. I will have those servants beaten. You may go back to your studies."

"Yes father, thank you," I leave the room as quickly as I can without appearing to run. I plan to be well into my studies when he has them beaten, so as there is no excuse for those beatings to expand to include me.

Eirene

* * *

I wake to that damned Dagma, touching my arm and swing out with that arm. I feel a great sense of satisfaction when I feel my hand connect with her face and hear the slap. "What are you doing in here touching me? How dare you! Why are you here?"

She snivels, "Please, ma'am, there is someone here. They

are asking for you and they said they won't leave till they have spoken with you personally."

"Well, who is it? Don't make me drag the information out of you! Do you need another slap to get it out?" I ask as I draw my hand up in preparation.

"No! No ma'am. It is Hulthen, from Sir Ingemar's estate. He says Sir Ingemar has sent him with urgent information and he must see you now."

My eyes narrow and I consider slapping her again. It won't do any good. The twit will just cry for the rest of the night and be even slower tomorrow. "Tell him I will be there shortly. Go!" I watch her scurry across the room and out the door, which she does remember to shut before she runs down the hall. Tossing the covers back, I set my feet to the warmed tile floor. I deserve more luxuries like this. That stupid husband of mine was always saying we shouldn't get ourselves too far above those that work for us, and he was always so stupid about these things. We are the ruling class for a reason. It took me years just to convince him we should have heated floors! Utter ridiculousness that it should take so long. Crossing the room, I take my robe from the chair I laid it on before I went to sleep. Slipping my arms into the cool silk, I smile, remembering that he is dead now and I don't have to concern myself with his ideas about how we should treat the lower classes.

Which is why I have a new silk robe and low-heeled slippers to go with it. Downstairs in the waiting room I find Hulthen, "Why has your master sent you here so late? What is it that couldn't wait until morning?"

Hulthen smirks, "My master sent me because your

daughter arrived at his home earlier this evening, with delusional tales of you attempting to wrest her inheritance away from her."

Damn the brat! I'll have her locked in the damn cellar until I can get this sorted. "Oh really? She has been unwell for quite some time. Did you not bring her with you?"

He looks away briefly and his smirk slips, "My master had her put in a room and unfortunately, she slipped away. We have people out searching for her right now. She should be safe at his manor before morning. Which brings me to the other business he wants to discuss with you. Ingemar would like to meet with you to discuss the possibility of a marriage between your daughter and his son."

Hm. So he plans for them to marry regardless whether or not I have anything to do with it. This could actually work out for me though, "Is he certain his son wants to marry her when she is so... unwell?"

"Yes," he nods, "he says that his son isn't really interested in a partner, but needs heirs. So if his wife is unwell, that is fine. She is physically healthy, yes?"

"Oh yes, quite healthy. Tell Ingemar I would love to discuss a wedding between our two children. I will expect to see him within the week. During the day, no midnight visits."

Hulthen nods and starts for the door saying, "I will relay your message, madame. I bid you good night."

Calling in the nearest guard, I tell him, "Valdís is out running the streets, go find her and bring her home."

Three

aldís

* * *

I haven't gone far when I hear the sounds of people searching for me. Taking off running as quietly as I can, heading for the city center. I headed that way anyway, because it will be morning soon, but now I need it for all the dark alleys and places to hide.

Ingemar's people are not taking me back there. His son is a creep, and he always has been. Now I know why. I am near the marketplace when I spy a convenient alley and I slow as I enter, letting my eyes adjust to the darker space as I move deeper into it. Nearly missing the little alcove and only seeing it because I hear the voices of Ingemar's guards and I turned to look at the entrance to the alley. I don't see them yet, but I duck into the alcove, pressing myself back into it as far as I can and slowing my breathing.

I hold my breath, pressing flat against the wall while they walk past me. They walk so slowly, but they aren't even looking around. I could have touched one as he walked past.

Forever or ten minutes later, I can see the sky beginning to lighten above me. People should start to move around soon. If I can stay hidden until then, blending into the morning crowd should be simple. It seems like time crawls by as I wait for the morning to get busy. But it does eventually. Merchants hawking their wares and people crowding the walks on their way to wherever they must go.

I move to the end of the alley and stand back in the shadows, observing for a few minutes. I don't see anyone that appears to be searching for anything beyond their next purchase. Stepping out, I weave into the crowd, blending in and moving farther away from my home and Ingemar's. I don't know what I am going to do yet, but getting farther away from those two places seems a safer bet.

Ingemar

* * *

Hulthen returned after I retired and so is here before my desk waiting for me to notice him so that he may give his report. I know already that my guards did not catch Valdís, I will send a better team after her shortly.

I take one last sip of my morning brew and acknowledge his presence. He bows before saying, "Madame Eirene has agreed to meet with you about the wedding of Pelos and Valdís. She was unaware that her daughter had left the premises and seemed quite annoyed by that. However, when I mentioned the offer of marriage, she was cheered by the idea."

Resting my elbows on the desk, I steeple my fingers over the mug, "How very interesting. And telling. Eirene's husband, recently and tragically dead, had switched heirs, going against the usual tradition and made his daughter the heir. Now the daughter shows up, talking about the mother trying to wrest her inheritance from her and deeply concerned about the welfare of her people. I feel like this will be useful information later. Tell no one what you have learned."

"Yes sir. Do you require anything else?"

"No, you may go about your duties. Tell the cook to send my breakfast in here this morning. I have some things to attend to."

Hulthen nods and backs quietly out of the room as I return to my notes.

Valdís

* * *

I wandered the market, getting myself a change of clothing along with a bag to carry the other clothes in. Before finding myself a vendor that sold breakfast sandwiches. Now I have a different, much warmer, set of clothing on and a hot sandwich, focus is a little easier. I find a rocky spot with a pleasant view that offers a seat tucked away from most eyes, and I climb up into it.

Folding the wrapper back from the sandwich, I take my first bite of cheesy, eggy goodness. It tastes so good. Ingemar was my only hope to keep my mother from stealing my inheritance. And inflicting cruelties upon the people we are supposed to care for, I don't know what I am going to do now.

I never made many friends outside of my home, so I have none of those that I could turn to. My father had one good friend, but that's only more trouble for me. Yuck! Pelos! Ew. I would never marry him, not for all the gold in the world. I realize I am staring at the castle in the distance. It is at the center of the city, on top of a small mountain. They say the mountain was formed by the Goddess from the terrible creature the kings fought to save our people. I don't know how true that is, but maybe the kings are the answer to my problem? I know they have a habit of killing people they feel are wasting their time with silly requests, but I don't know where else to turn.

This really is a matter that could affect the entire kingdom over time. I guess I'll do it. They can't be that bad and they are meant to protect us, to protect the people of this land. I guess if they think I am just a silly girl, they will kill me and my part in the problem will be solved. Having decided my fate, I get up and dust myself off. Now I just need to figure out how I am getting to the castle.

Climbing out of my little hiding spot, I see some of Ingemar's guards wandering the market. Great. Just what I need. I walk away from them and spot a hire car. I walk a little faster and get to the driver's window, "Are you available?"

He looks up, surprised, "Yes. Where you want to go?"

"The castle."

"That's going to be a good fifty, but hop in."

I step back and get into the back seat of the car. He starts the car and has us going almost as soon as I close the door. I look behind us as I hear shouts and I see Ingemar's guards. They definitely saw me. The driver sees them as well and asks, "Friends of yours?"

"No, definitely not my friends."

"You aren't running from the law, right?"

"No. Running from an unwanted suitor."

He makes a face in the mirror, saying, "Sounds unpleasant. The guy just isn't taking no for an answer, huh?"

"He isn't. He is a very unpleasant sort."

"Well, if that is what you are going to the castle about, I suppose he will leave you alone. One way or another." With that ominous comment, my driver fell silent for the rest of the trip.

Four

V aldís

* * *

The drive to the castle is long, no matter how you get there. With my driver silent, all I am left with are my thoughts. The coming petition to the kings weighs heavily on my mind. The kings take turns ruling, with only one of them awake and dealing with the world at any one time. I know the king over them all, King Vincent, never wanted anything to do with ruling and he won't even see petitioners during the times when he is the king in place. But he isn't the one in place right now.

Right now, King Knox is our king in place. He is the most willing of the five kings left to hear petitions. Admittedly, that has made him the king that has killed the most petitioners as well, but it looks like that is due more to volume than his potential for violence.

King Malic will be next after him. He is less willing to tolerate humans. Rumor has it that because he is the biggest of them all and strongest, he was a protector of the kings and hasn't forgiven himself for the deaths of the other kings. As it was humans that killed them, his patience for us is less, though we differ slightly from the humans that murdered the other kings.

King Chance was the hunter, and if I recall correctly, he was the one that hunted the murderers still on the island after things calmed down. He is the one that makes petitioners fear even the accidental appearance of guilt or lies. He watches everything and judges it all with lightning speed.

King Gage is rumored to be part animal. His eyes are a golden color that looks more like they came from a wolf than anything else. He smells people and tells their darkest secrets based on their scent. Of all of them, he is the creepiest by far and his ability to sniff things out has caused a lot of scandal. But only because people had things to hide. There was one instance I heard about where a petitioner was claiming someone had stolen his wife and raped her. King Gage came down from his throne and walked around the three. At the completion of a circuit around them, he grabbed the husband by the throat and called him out for his lies. He told everyone present that day that the man had been brutalizing his wife and the only scent on her was his. He even knew whose child she carried. It was the talk of the city for ages after he killed the man.

. . .

The castle is a lot bigger in person. The hire car lets me out in front of the main entrance. He gives me his card and says, "If you make it out of here, call our office and they will send me. I am one of the few willing to come up here."

I thank him as I pay him, and he pulls away. Left alone, I turn to face the castle. It is dark. There are terrifying stone creatures all over the place. I am still taking them in when the door opens, and a man steps out, "Do you plan to gawk at the castle for the rest of the day, or did you intend to come in?"

My mouth snaps shut. I didn't realize it was hanging open. "Ye-," I clear my throat and try again, "Yes, please. I do intend to come in. My apologies, it is a sight."

He looks around, doubtful. "I suppose it is if this is your first time. Is this your first time being here?"

Walking toward him and he turns to lead me into the castle as I tell him, "Yes. I never had a reason to come here before and I do now and I just wasn't expecting... well, any of it. I don't know what to expect. Honestly, I'm just hoping for a miracle."

He stops and looks at me with what might be pity before he turns to shut the door. Then the scent hits me. Inhaling deeply, I take in as much of it as I can. It smells so good. I can't quite place it, though. It makes me hot and yearning but also comforted? "What is that amazing smell?"

The man looks like I have lost my mind. "I am certain I don't know what smell you are referring to. The cook isn't even starting dinner preparations yet. My name is Epaphras. I am the go-to person around here. Let us go to the study and discuss why exactly you are here."

I nod and follow him to a cozy room with a desk and tables overflowing with papers. He motions for me to sit as he seats himself on the other side of the desk. "Now, tell me, why you are here and what exactly you hope to happen if you are allowed audience with the king in place."

I tell him everything about my mother, my father, my suspicions about how he died, and what Ingemar tried to do when I went there for aid. "As for what I hope for, well, I just want the people we are meant to take care of to be safe and well cared for. If that costs me my life, I'll consider it a fair price. And if I am allowed to live, I would really like to not marry Ingemar's son Pelos. He really is awful."

Epaphras had taken up a pen and prepared to work on some papers while listening to me, but he never put pen to paper and he just sat there staring as I told him all of it. As I finish, he swallows and shakes his head, "Well then. I suppose you do need to be seen." He stands and walks around the desk, gesturing for me to stand and follow him. "I am going to take you to a room. There are a lot of rules for meeting with the kings. The current king in place is King Knox. I miss the old names. They sounded so much more dignified. I digress. You will need to dress more femi-nine, more suited for court. Spare me the reasons for your pants and shirt attire. They don't matter. I am telling you what will help your case with King Knox. Please, whatever you do, do not display any sort of attraction to the king. That never goes well." He stops and turns to look at me, brows raised.

Taking the opportunity, I ask him, "You really don't smell that?"

He scowls, "No! Have you been listening?"

I scowl right back, "Yes! King Knox, dress, not having the visible hots for the king. That smell is really distracting, though. You really can't smell it?"

"No, I can't smell it. Focus!" He turns and leads the way up the stairs, telling me, "The king is likely to end you if you make any attraction to him known. Don't wear anything terribly revealing. There is clothing in the wardrobe in a variety of sizes and styles. Something should suit you. Have no fear, it is all quite clean. We donate anything that has been worn if the wearer does not take it home with them."

"Out of curiosity, if the king doesn't want any attraction to him displayed, why does it matter what I wear?"

Epaphras gives me a side-eye as he stops in front of a door and unlocks it, saying, "It matters because you want him in a disposition to help you and not kill you. Personally, I hate the mess when he kills the petitioners. Now, I will leave you here. Nearly everything you should need will be in here, do pull the cord if you need anything else."

I nod and wander into the room. He closes the door behind me. The room is gorgeous, an enormous bed dominates the center of the room. The promised wardrobe is off to one side and the biggest monstrosity of a piece of furniture that I have ever seen. I wander through the door at the other end, and into that bathroom. There is a huge soaking tub just begging for someone to have a bath and I am that someone.

. . .

Knox

* * *

The never ending stacks of paperwork are somewhat smaller now that I have been at them for three hours. Why is there so damn much paper work to running a country? I hear Epaphras walking to the door and I tell him to come in before he can knock. I hate that sound.

"Good afternoon, my King. I have terrible news for you."

My shoulders drop. I only have a little longer before one of my brothers-in-arms, my fellow kings, arrives home to take over the running of the kingdom and I can go wander the world. Easing the loneliness and slaking the lust that has always plagued me. My brothers and I never do either of those here on the island. The last time we did was so disastrous as to be comical. "What is this terrible news you have for me, Epaphras?"

He smiles, and it is too happy. My eyes narrow as I watch him telling me, "Well, Sire, there is a very odd petitioner here. They do have quite the set of problems and I feel certain that if they are not taken care of, it will affect the kingdom as a whole."

Too much set up. This feels like a trap. "Get to the point Epaphras. You know I hate overly long stories."

He swallows, "Erm, yes. Paperwork has put you in a mood, I see." He backs toward the door, saying, "They are in a room so you can see them tomorrow. I can just—"

"Get on with it, I would rather know now."

He stops and sighs, "Very well. Conrí Potentus died not long ago. Strangely enough, he had an extended illness prior to his death. After which he changed his will so that his eldest daughter would inherit as opposed to the still living wife and mother to the eldest. That didn't kick off an investigation because sometimes people do strange things with no explanation." He pauses and starts to pace, saying, "But now the daughter is here. She says her mother is working to wrest the inheritance from her. She says she escaped her home and went to the home of her father's oldest friend, Sir Ingemar. Ingemar decided that marrying her to his son Pelos against her will would solve all her problems. She escaped there and, after a rather harrowing morning, made her way here to seek what she termed a miracle." He stops his pacing and turns to look at me, his face screwed up with concern, "All that is something you can fix. I feel certain of this. The odd thing is that since she has been here, from the minute she walked in, she has been smelling something. She can't or won't describe it, but it seems to almost mesmerize her."

The last sentences, the oddness he describes, strike an icy chord of terror in my chest. It can't be. Not after all this time. It was just a story the Goddess told us to give us hope through the long millennia. It's not possible that Conrí Potentus's eldest daughter is the one she told us about. Just the idea makes me want to run out and smell the castle, pick up her scent and see if it has the same effect on me. My anger grows as I realize she must have heard the stories from her father and is trying to become queen. I shake my head at the audacity of this woman, saying, "I will see her tomorrow as you have her in a room. How are the preparations for my journey coming? I will want to leave the minute Malic arrives."

Epaphras flinches when I snarl at him, and I regret losing my control. He recovers before I can say anything and says, "We have the boat nearly ready. The supplies are ready to load. Have you decided where you will go this time?"

I can't help but feel grateful that Epaphras understands so well and forgives so easily, as he says, "Thank you. No, I haven't decided yet. None of the places I think about visiting seems quite right. Maybe I am just apathetic about it all. Perhaps I should go to Italy. Eat pasta and drink from well-fed and half drunk tourists for a time." Only that doesn't feel right either, and I have this terrible feeling that I won't be going anywhere.

Five

V aldís

* * *

Last night's dinner tray is gone when I wake. Someone must have come to get it while I slept. It is such a weird thing, that I was able to sleep so deeply here when I could never at my home. My home, the place where I should have felt the most safe and relaxed. Yet, here in this castle where I may very well die later today, here I relax so deeply that I sleep through someone entering the room to collect dishes. Shaking my head, I slip out of the bed and head for the bathroom.

A quick shower later and I get dressed for the day. Whatever happens today, I am going to go out there as myself. Besides, the scent in this place is driving me to distraction. It is less in this room, but it is still here. But the scent permeates the castle. It smells of dreams and lost things and lust, so much lust. My pussy has been throbbing with need since I first smelled it, and it hasn't ceased. I have never felt so in need of being railed right now.

By the time I am fully dressed, I am starving. I go to the door and find the fucking thing is locked. Those bastards! How dare they! Why? Deciding I need to think this through as best I can, considering that I am well on my way to hangry, I try to focus. Besides being ridiculously horny. I seat myself at the small table I ate at last night. Why? Why lock a petitioner in their room? I think about what he told me yesterday. Something he said tickles my memory... Something about not displaying attraction for the king. Yes! I am certain that's it. Don't display attraction and then he locks me in my room. Oh, no. Oh. How many women threw themselves at the kings before it got like this? How many women snuck out of their rooms and did awful things before they started locking women in their rooms? I still want to be mad but, I just don't have anything to put behind it now that I have a pretty good idea of why.

Hangry however, that I have in plenty. By the time my door opens, I am pacing with vigor as my stomach tries to eat its way through my spine. "Finally! I am so hungry!"

The same man from yesterday enters the room, saying, "My apologies. I intended to be here much earlier, but was kept away by other responsibilities."

My anger is mostly gone, knowing he was trying to get here though I am still growly, I tell him, "It's fine. Can we get me something to eat now?"

He grins when I say that, "Yes, of course. Come with me."

He leads me to a small room set with a spread for breakfast and I sit where he indicates much faster than propriety says is okay. I can't bring myself to care, though, and I dig into the dishes with gusto. He pours our island's strong root brew into two cups, silently pushing one toward me as he seats himself in the chair across from me. He stares out the window while sipping his brew until my eating slows. "Tell me about yourself, Valdís."

"What do you want to know?"

"Do you still smell the scent you kept asking me about?"

I glare at him, checking to see if he is suggesting I might be crazy. He doesn't seem to be, so I tell him, "I do. I could smell it in my sleep even. Do you have any idea what it might be? I've never smelled anything like this."

He shakes his head lightly, saying, "No. I'm sorry, I do not. No one has ever had this problem in all this time. Why do you think your father made you his heir?"

Setting my fork down, I say, "I only have suspicions. Nothing concrete and nothing verifiable. My father fell very ill for a long time. No one could figure out what was wrong with him. He went, in a space of weeks, from a happy and hale man to an invalid. It baffled his doctors. Then one day, he issued orders about his food and drink. Only certain people could prepare his food, and it was never to be left unattended. Ever. He began to get well after that and I had deep suspicions about my mother. She was one of the people that my father forbade to have anything to do with his food preparation."

He nods, "I see. Remind me, please, how did your father die?"

"He received a message that some of our people were in need of aid with a broken machine. They requested him specifically and stated that the machine may need to be replaced. He was murdered while he was on the way there. My mother has been working to convince everyone that my father had an accident. I saw his body. Accidents don't leave multiple stab wounds or slit your throat. I kept the note requesting his presence. And I sent someone loyal to me out to see about the machine. The people the note was to have been from did not write it, nor did they have any broken machinery."

"I see. Have you finished eating?" I nod and he stands, telling me, "Come. I will take you to the waiting room. You will be there until we come to get you for the audience."

Knox

Epaphras is an exemplary employee. But if he doesn't stop talking, I might choke him. My state clothing feels slightly confining. Tugging at the neckline does nothing beyond popping threads, no matter how gentle I think I am being. I can smell her in the castle and the scent of her has me feeling things I am not interested in feeling. Not for anyone on this island. No matter how I keep telling myself, it won't be long before Malic gets here and I can go. I'll just tell Epaphras to put off any further petitions until Malic gets here. I can make it through this last one, no matter how she smells like I need to take her and make her mine.

Rolling my shoulders, I stop before the door to the throne room. Epaphras gives me a questioning look, his hand on the doorknob and I tell him, "I'm ready. Go get her and let's get this over with."

He opens the door and bows out of the way, saying, "Yes, sire."

I walk in and close the door behind me. The room is empty. Crossing to the throne, I look down at it. We covered it with the skin of the creature we killed so long ago. The Goddess said we must keep it and use it in this manner to keep her people mindful that they would not be here without us. I hate it, but she is our goddess. What am I going to do? Tell her no? Ha! I'm sure that would go over well. Turning, I seat myself. The throne room is too big, but in times past we had many more here. We allowed the nobles into our lives more.

Then they showed us how duplicitous they could be and we stopped the practice. That was over a hundred years ago. There are still many nobles around that remember that period. While we became vampires to protect our people and gained immortality, the Goddess granted her subjects a longer than average life span. Most of our people living at least a couple hundred years.

The door at the other end of the room opens and

Epaphras leads the woman into the room. Her scent hits me and my cock springs to life, painfully hard. My teeth drop as if I were going to drink, and it takes great effort to pull them back as they walk across the room. I want to take her now, to protect her from all things. This isn't possible! The story was just a story. She didn't mean that we would actually have someone. This is a fluke. I can control myself. She needs protection only as a subject, not as mine.

Even thinking the word mine sends a shiver through my body and I work to control it enough that they won't see. They stop before me and she curtsies in her pants outfit. I guess she ignored Epaphras' warning to dress feminine. I like it. No! Don't like it. Get this over with so you can retreat to your rooms. I grate out, "I will hear your petition now."

Epaphras raises a brow as he moves off to one side. I ignore him, focus my attention on the delicious woman before me as she begins to speak. Her voice is soothing. It eases me in ways I didn't know were possible. Her story really is awful, but I can't smell a trace of a lie on her. She could be wrong, but it would be easy enough to check all of her story. A single tear slips down her face as she tells me about her father's death. I clench my hands around the arms of the throne. Everything in me wants to scoop her up and kiss her tears and her problems away after I kill all those that have ever wronged her. My fingers are digging into the arms of the throne. Splintering the wood under the beast's skin as she tells me about Ingemar's treatment of her when she sought help there first.

I will end him and his son if they ever touch her again.

She has finished her petition by asking only that I ensure her mother cannot harm her people. That's it. Nothing else. I can see her nostrils flaring. She is scenting me and I know it is causing her to be heavily aroused. I see my face reflected in her eyes. I look angry. But I smell no fear on her as she awaits my response. If I give her a judgement, she will leave. I don't want her to leave. I can't let her go yet. Standing, I tell her, "Stay another night. I will see you again tomorrow."

I smell her anger and fight back a smile as I turn and leave the room. I can hear her telling Epaphras, "This is garbage. Why does he need me here another day?"

As I open the door and exit the room, Epaphras says, "I don't know. This has never happened before."

Eirene

* * *

Today is the day Ingemar comes to discuss the wedding of our children. He has always been a tiresome sort of man. Though that may have been my dear departed husband's influence if recent events are to be believed. I have dressed carefully. I am still in mourning, as far as the public is concerned. Dagma comes to let me know Ingemar is in the study. I nod and tell her to bring us refreshments as I leave the room and make my way to the study.

Telling the guards to stand outside, I seat myself behind the desk so well loved by Conrí. "Hello Ingemar. Tell me, what is your proposal regarding the marriage of our children?"

He raises a brow, seeming mildly taken aback at my directness. "Good to see you as well, Eirene. As for our children, I believe a marriage between our children would benefit everyone. Our houses have always been close and this would unite them. Then there are all those very messy accusations from your daughter. I feel certain it would be better for you if those not get out. We are prepared to work with you in ensuring that the rest of the world believes your daughter to be addled in some way. Perhaps the death of her father has unhinged her? My son needs heirs and a wife to provide them. His wife does not need to be a partner in every sense of the word. His wife would stay confined within the walls of our home, as my wife has all these long years."

With a chuckle, I ask him, "How exactly will you manage that, when you could not hold her for even one night?"

He scowls, saying, "That was a mistake that will not be repeated. A careless servant that will not be so careless ever again."

A knock sounds at the door. I answer, saying, "Come in."

Dagma comes to stand at the side of the desk, saying, "I apologize for interrupting your meeting, but one of the people sent out after Valdís has returned and you said you wanted to know right away."

"Yes, yes, get on with it!" I hiss at the ignorant woman.

"They said that she was seen going to the castle. They

didn't see her actually go in, but they did see the hire car take her up there and come back empty."

"Hmm, is that all you have for me?" She nods and whispers yes madam, "Good. Get out."

Dagma shuffles her way out the door while we wait for it to close behind her. Once it finally closes, I look at Ingemar, saying, "I think this could work in our favor. If we can convince the king in place that she is delusional and have her remanded to our custody, it would solve both our problems."

He nods, bringing a hand up to stroke his own chin, saying, "Of course, it could be just as convenient if she were to die at the castle. Likely very profitable, as we could sue the king for damages. We need to convince the world that we had always intended for our children to marry and unite the houses. I can have documents created that appear to have been signed by Conrí many years ago. Stating that our children will wed at... oh, say sixty, and we will spread it about that we had been postponing the affair in hopes that Valdís would return to herself."

I feel the smile spreading across my face, and tell him, "I like it. She will be insanely mad about the entire idea and the only ones that would contradict it are servants. If they know what is good for them, they will keep quiet. No one asks questions when the servants go missing. Except Conrí, but he's not here anymore. Yes, that will work. Go get those documents prepped. Send them by and I will sign them both before returning one copy to you. We should leave soon for the castle, to seek our wayward Valdís. How soon can you have this done?"

"Very," he says as he stands. "I will send it, and why don't you bring it back when you are on your way to the castle? We will ride together and present a united front to the king in place."

"I like it. I will await the documents. Would you like someone to show you out?"

He laughs, "No, I fair recall the way."

Ingemar

* * *

Leaving Conrí's estate, I find my car parked in the circle drive. My driver has an excellent sense of when to arrive, and I climb in the back while he holds the door open for me. I tell him, "Take us home."

Once the car begins to move, I turn to my son Pelos, "We will need to tread cautiously. You will marry Valdís as soon as we can get the little bitch out of the castle. Once we have her, the wedding will proceed immediately and then you get to work making sure she is pregnant. Until she is delivered of a healthy child, you will not strike her. You will also try to avoid marking her in general."

Pelos nods his understanding, "Father, once she has had the child, may I do with her as I please?"

"Yes, of course. Though you must make sure that things look accidental in case of questions."

Pelos smiles as he nods and turns to look out the window. That boy may have to have an accident once I have

36

another heir. Perhaps I should visit her occasionally as well, to double the chances of her getting pregnant. Yes, I think I will. After all, I have proven I can fertilize a woman's womb. He, however, has been plowing everything he could get to stand still long enough and has yet to have a single child wandering about claiming parentage fees. Who knows if he even can father a child? Better to just ensure it will be a child of my line. Once we have that child, I can sue for dear Valdís's inheritance. The inheritance wrested away by her hateful mother. Yes, that will work nicely, as I am only protecting the interests of my grandchild...

Eirene

* * *

Eumeleia enters the study shortly after Ingemar leaves, "Wonderful, come, have a drink with me, darling one. I have spectacular news."

She smiles and goes directly to the drink cabinet. Pouring a glass of golden wine for each of us, handing mine over before taking her seat across the desk from me, "What is this news you have, mother?"

A quick sip of my wine and I tell her, "We have found Valdís, she is at the castle. Once she is returned to us, we will marry her off to Ingemar's son Pelos," I see her blanch. She thinks I don't know how she feels about him, but she needs to forget the idea. I continue on, saying, "and while all that is going on, I will be quietly having her disinherited for reasons of mental instability. It is perfect! She will be fully disinherited, meaning no one will be able to come back later and steal her inheritance away from us for any of her offspring. It will all be yours one day, as I always intended."

"I see," she sips her wine, "and Pelos is fine with this plan? Did anyone consult him?"

"Oh yes, his father has spoken for him and they are quite close. It will be a quick and quiet wedding. We plan to spread the rumor that they were always intended to be married. It has only been her mental instability holding them back, and what a sweet boy he is for taking her on as his wife, knowing that he will never have a true partner in her."

I watch with narrowed eyes as she downs the rest of her glass and she says, "It sounds as though everything is planned out perfectly. I am suddenly not feeling well Mother, I think I will go lie down for a time."

"Yes dear, lie down and get right with this plan. We are securing your future here. Mourn the boy if you must, but then let him go and concern yourself with only your future."

Her shoulders slump a bit as she says, "Yes, Mother. I am just tired. I will be down for dinner."

"Oh, I don't know if I will be here for that. Perhaps you should take dinner in your rooms this evening?"

She stops with a hand on the doorknob and her head bowed, saying, "Yes Mother, I will do that. I am sure it will help with this awful headache. Thank you."

"You are so welcome. Come, give your mother a kiss before you go."

She trudges across the room, kisses my cheek, and immediately turns to head for the door. I don't stop her this time. There is no point. She will have to have her mope before she can get herself together. I know it as well as she does. A damn shame she likes that boy so much. He's really quite dreadful.

Six

V aldís

* * *

The stunned feeling isn't going away as Epaphras leads me back to the room I spent last night in. I want this king more than I have ever wanted anyone in my entire life. The anger in him only excited me more. What is wrong with me? This is not a normal reaction. Was his reaction normal? Epaphras looks a little shocked, too. Maybe I am not the only one affected? No! No way the king was affected by me. That is just ridiculous. I am nobody. My own mother doesn't want me. There is no way he does.

Epaphras startles me from my thoughts when he says, "No one has ever stayed here more than one night. Not since they stopped the parties. Who are you?"

Shrugging, I tell him, "No one. Just Conrí Potentus's

unwanted daughter. What do you mean, no one stays here more than one night? No one? Really? Is he going to kill me while I sleep? Will he still help my people after I am dead?"

Epaphras laughs loudly, stopping in the hall to clutch his belly with one hand and keep himself upright with the other on the wall. I cross my arms and lean against the wall a little away from him, lips twisted with annoyance. All the laughter is uncalled for. He regains control of himself and says, "My apologies. I don't usually laugh at guests. It just struck me as hilarious. The way you were so matter of fact about the possibility of the king coming to murder you in your sleep and at the same time, concerned for your people's welfare. Come, let's keep going. To answer your questions, if the king were going to kill you, it would have happened in the throne room. We would be cleaning up the mess of you still. He has no intention of killing you. As for your people, I feel certain he intends to at least look into things as they are his people, too. He may not enjoy dealing with the business of ruling, but he does care for the people of this island."

We have arrived at the door to my room and I ask him, "Are you going to lock me in again?"

He nods, "Yes, I am. I will be back for you at dinner and I will sit with you while you eat, so you have some company. Until then, is there anything I can get you?"

"No. I'll be fine until dinner. I noticed there are some books. Maybe I'll have another bath."

"Excellent, I will come for you at dinner then." He

closes the door behind me and I can hear his footsteps, near running down the hall.

Knox

* * *

I hear Epaphras running to my quarters and my eyes roll involuntarily. I still can't get the scent of her out of my mind. It's all I can do to stay away from her. I can't tell Epaphras he doesn't need to get his hopes up. He is stopped outside the doors to my quarters trying to get himself together. I call out, "Just come in already."

He opens the door and peers around it, his face still lightly flushed, saying, "Sire." He walks a bit closer, though he stays a healthy distance away, saying, "I don't mean to question your decisions, but why are we keeping her here another day? Are we going to be investigating her problems? The mother does sound problematic in so many ways. And there is the question of whether or not she had her husband murdered, whether she might decide to do the same to Valdís..."

The idea of Valdís's mother attempting to kill her sends rage and blood lust coursing through my body. If I don't calm down, I'll have to have an extra pint today. "And that is why she must stay here as we conduct an investigation into what the mother is up to, and Ingemar as well. I want him thoroughly investigated. Go, send people out to handle that." I start to turn away when I realize she will be here for dinner, saying, "Wait. Set the table for two. I'll take my dinner with her."

Epaphras' jaw drops and I head for the study that is part of my suite of rooms. I know I have work to do in there. I hear him leave the room as I sit down and I breathe a sigh of relief.

* * *

Valdís

* * *

The door to my room flies open, and I jump. Epaphras runs in. His eyes are wide and his hair looks like he ran the length of the castle as he shouts at me, "You have to bathe and dress! Please wear a dress this time? Please?"

"What? Why?"

He is heaving, still trying to catch his breath. Maybe he did run the length of the castle? He straightens and takes a deep inhale, saying, "The king, he plans to have dinner with you. He has never had dinner alone with anyone the entire time I have worked here. I don't know what this means exactly, but he is taking an interest in you."

My brows drop, I ask, "Why? I'm nobody. My mother doesn't even want me. I am in shock that the king is even willing to speak to me when it seems like all I do is piss him off."

Epaphras is only panting a little as he says, "What do you mean?"

"Couldn't you smell it? He was angry during the audience. The poor throne is going to need some serious repair after what he did to the arms."

"You could smell that he was angry?"

"Yes! Couldn't you? It felt like the room was saturated with his anger. And that smell. You know, it was a lot stronger in there. You should check the throne room for weird items lying around."

His brows are raised as he says, "Indeed. We will go over the room and see if we can find anything. In the meantime, get showered. I will find you something appropriate to wear. Please say you will wear it? For me?"

I march off to the bathroom, making no promises. If he pulls out some giant cupcake of a thing, I will not ever put that on my body. It would mean a broken promise. My shower is quick and perfunctory. After I dry, I spend some time pressing most of the water from my hair. Putting on my underthings and wrapping a towel over those, I leave the bathroom to see what he has chosen.

He is sitting in a chair and stands when I enter the room and says, "Excellent, you will look at least. Thank you. Now, I picked three different ensembles. I know you are nobility as well, so fewer worries about you dropping food down your front due to all the training you likely received. Starting with red, black, and white. I think any of them would be stunning on you."

I nod and study the dresses. A black dress has silver spaghetti straps and a low slung slouch neckline, the rest of the dress being mostly fitted. The red dress is also fitted and has long sleeves and a keyhole opening over the chest. The white looks like the top is split into two pieces with only a thin bit of silver holding them together, and a skirt that appears to be mostly two panels of cloth that overlap near the top. I look over at Epaphras, "I thought the rule was that we didn't want me to dress sexy?"

He shrugs, saying, "The rules are changing. We must change with them. Hence, my choices of dress."

"I see. I don't know what to choose. Until now, I always had to look frumpy next to my mother and sister or face the consequences. Um, can you help me choose?"

His brows scrunch down and he seems annoyed but then closes his eyes and takes a breath, saying, "I'll just file that information away for later questions. Are you more comfortable in fitted clothing or loose? Judging by your wardrobe thus far, fitted. But I don't know if that applies to dresses as well."

"I usually wore looser clothing so as not to show off what mother termed my lumps."

"Lumps? Oh, Sweet Goddess. Your mother is a piece of work. Take the white dress and go try it on."

He hands over the dress and I retreat to the bathroom. Once the door is closed, I drop my towel and realize the bra has to go. It is old and ragged and will not work under this dress. Making quick work of the fastenings, I drop the bra to the floor, too. Slipping the dress over my head, I have to pull the waist down over my boobs. From there, it falls to rest at the top of my hips. A little rearranging and everything seems to be covered. Walking out of the bathroom, I hear Epaphras gasp and I say, "Oh no, is it that bad? I'll go change."

He shrieks, "No," and runs over to grab my wrist, "It looks that good. I knew you had a splendid figure, but I had no idea it would be so complimented by this dress. No, you look magnificent. Now, let's accent the rest of you."

V aldís

* * *

Epaphras escorts me to a large dining room where the king is waiting for me. The king is waiting for me? What is this planet I have landed on? I don't understand. He turns as we walk toward him and he smiles at me. The king is smiling at me. So, of course, that is the very moment when my heel lands wrong, my ankle wobbles and I start to fall. Before I can hit the ground, his highness is next to me and catches me, asking, "Are you all right?"

My face burning with embarrassment, I tell him, "I— yes. I'm fine. I'm sorry. Thank you." He is still holding me just a foot or so from the ground, his eyes... I can't think straight, and that scent is overwhelming. Oh no. It is the king. The scent is the king. Oh, fuck me. "I, um, I should, shouldn't we stand?"

King Knox looks surprised that we aren't and lifts us smoothly back to upright. It's a little dizzying. He keeps a hand on my arm to steady me and guides me to my seat. Then the king pulls my chair out for me and seats me himself before he sits in the chair at the end of the table. I am sitting in the very first seat to the right of him. What does all this mean? Why is he being so nice? His reputation for killing petitioners is so at odds with everything that has happened here today. Especially this. Epaphras is gone, and another employee walks in, serving us with a soup. I watch in amazement as they place some of the soup in the dish before the king. Do the kings eat food? I pick up my spoon and dip it into the soup carefully, watching the king as he does the same.

He brings the spoon to his lips and takes it in his mouth, his lips wrapping around the spoon. Maybe I should not be watching this, as I have a sudden sharp desire to be a spoon. Eyes on my own spoon, I try to focus on eating and not spilling any of the soup on myself. He must have noticed my incredibly awkward silence and guessed at the reason. He chuckles and says, "We all eat actual food. Does everyone not know that about us? Scratch that. What does everyone think about us?"

"Hm, do you really want to know?"

He smiles at me, and my heart stops beating for a second. "Yes, I really want to know. We don't get out much here."

"Well. You have a reputation for killing petitioners that displease you somehow."

He nods as they clear away our soup bowls and bring

the next course in, saying, "That is fair. We do kill petitioners that ask awful things or are perpetrating crimes against our people using a thin layer of the letter of the law. We have no tolerance for lies or games."

"And I am told that women displaying attraction to you often die as well."

He shakes his head ruefully, saying, "That may be a little ill informed. Yes, we do sometimes kill them, but only if they are behaving poorly and not respecting our boundaries."

This time I am nodding, telling him, "That seems fair. Everyone thinks that you all take turns sleeping here in the castle. One rules, the others sleep."

He eyes me, asking, "And what do you think?"

"I think you are the only one in residence because of the scent. If you were all here would probably drive me to insanity." As soon as the words leave my lips, I know they are a mistake.

He lifts his brows, saying, "The scent?"

"Erm, I don't suppose we could just forget that I said anything, could we?"

"No." He looks almost like he is angered by my desire to not tell him.

"Fine. As soon as I walked into the castle, I could smell this scent. It is a very nice," exceedingly sexy, "scent, and I find it quite distracting." The scent of you makes me want to taste every inch of you. It smells so damn good. I barely know what to do with myself, and my panties are constantly damp around you. "I realized it was you when you caught me just a bit ago. Until then, I had suspicions after the audience earlier."

He smiles, saying, "You find the scent of me distracting?"

My face is searing hot again, as I say, "Yes." I turn my eyes away from him. It is just too much. Is this dinner ever going to end? Turning my eyes back to my food, I take a bite so I have something to really focus on.

After swallowing that bite I risk a glance at King Knox through my lashes, he is focused on his food. Exhaling a breath I didn't realize I had been holding, I continue eating, grateful that he is willing to let that go. All too soon, the dinner is finished. The king stands and I stand with him, waiting for him to leave the room so I can leave as well, but he walks to my chair and slides it away, gesturing for me to come with him. What is he doing? "What are you doing?"

He scowls at me, saying, "I am walking you back to your room. Get away from the table before I decide to put you where I really want you."

Stepping away, because I'm not willing to test that theory, I tell him, "You aren't supposed to be doing this for me. And what do you mean, put me where you want me? You are the one flouting the damn social mores?"

He narrows his eyes at me and leans in toward me, growling out, "Because I am the king and I do what I damn well please. You would do well to remember that."

Oh, fuck him. I'll find a different way to do things. "Fuck you. I don't give a fucking damn what you please, as long as it doesn't involve me. Good night." I walk away as his jaw hangs and I can feel him watching me. My retreat is going great right up till I trip over the carpet and go flying. I land face first in something that smells amazing and shit, he has caught me again. Pushing against his chest, the smirk on his face is irritating me further. I am so done. I tell him as I put a hand on his arm, "Let me fix this so you don't have to save me again." Keeping hold of his arm, his fantastically thick arm, I lean down and snatch my shoes off one at a time. Straightening, I remove my hand from his arm, saying, "I didn't want to wear these to begin with, anyway. Thanks for catching me, now fuck off to whatever you damn well please."

Striding off down the hall, my steps only falter slightly when he seems to be next to my ear as he says, "That dress looks great on you." When I turn to shove him away, the hall is empty.

Epaphras comes toward me as I stride toward my room, "Where are you going? Why are you not with the king?"

"Because he told me I should remember that he does whatever he damn well pleases and it pissed me off."

He sighs, saying, "Let's get you to your room."

The sun has set, and I have changed into my own clothes, all the makeup washed away. The room feels close and confining. I find a set of doors behind some curtains and a balcony beyond that. Stepping out, I see some of the most gorgeous gardens I have ever seen. The longing to wander through them and enjoy a communion with the plants hits me, sharp like a knife. Moving to the edge of the balcony, I look down; it isn't that far. I won't be able to sneak back in by any means unless they have a ladder that folds down really small and is so lightweight that I could pull it up. Chances of that? Zero. So, now the question is, do I hop down and take the consequences or do I remain in here like a good girl?

"You are going to hurt yourself if you jump from there."

His voice floats up, and I jump. Looking down, I see King Knox standing at the edge of the garden, looking very know it all. "I can make it down from here just fine, thank you. I was just debating on whether I wanted to face the consequences if I do so because I don't see a good way to get back in."

He raises a brow at me, saying, "Oh really? You think you can get down from the second story without injuring yourself?"

Grinning, I tell him, "I know I can. I told you, my only reason for pausing is a question of consequences."

He laughs, "Ok, let's see you do it. If you make it down without injuring yourself, I will take you on a guided tour of the gardens. If you injure yourself, I will take you to the doctor."

Narrowing my eyes at him, I ask, "Will there be any consequences for being out of my room? You aren't going to say I was wandering around hunting you or something, are you?"

His brows drop, he asks, "What? No. Why would I?"

"I am confined to this room, so you don't have to concern yourself with women wandering about trying to catch you and become queen or some shit. I have enough problems without making you one of them, thank you very much. If I want someone to be mean to me, I can just go home."

His face is dark when I finish speaking. He says, "No. You will have no consequences. I sought you out. Come, you may walk through the castle if you like, and I will show you the gardens."

I grin, "No way am I walking through the castle when there is this lovely balcony crying out for me to defeat it." Having said that, I throw a leg over the side of the balcony and start the process. Once my body is outside the balcony, I start with lowering myself to hanging from the balcony, very close to the wall so I can use it for leverage. Once I am hanging from the bottom, I move away from the wall a bit. When I get near the corner, I turn around and swing my body back and forth, not for speed so much as momentum. When I have just the right amount of swing, I let go on the out swing and roll through the landing, coming up to my feet with a flourish. I hear King Knox clapping softly behind me and I turn, offering a deep bow. "Thank you, thank you. For my next trick, I get to wander the lovely gardens and not get in trouble for leaving the claustrophobic confines of my room."

He walks over and holds an arm bent at the elbow out toward me. I look up at him, unsure. Should I be on the arm of the king? If this goes badly, he won't be the one to suffer the consequences, I tell him, "I don't think I should. If someone sees me displaying such familiarity with you, it could go badly for me."

His brows and the corners of his lovely mouth drop

into a scowl, as he says, "If anyone gives you any grief of any sort about this, I will end them. Take my arm. Please."

"Ending them seems a little much, but I guess with reassurance like that how can I say no?" The breeze turns as I slip my hand onto his arm and I smell that scent again. Liquid fire runs through my body as my pussy throbs in response. Clamping my jaw, I manage not to moan, but I do stumble a bit.

The king looks down at the ground but keeps walking, a slow smile on his lips. He leads me down the path toward the lilacs. They aren't in bloom right now, but the bushes are still lovely. As we enter the herb garden, he speaks over the buzzing of the bees, saying, "Tell me about your life."

I raise a brow, asking, "What would you like to know?"

"Tell me about your relationship with your father."

"Well, he was a good, if sometimes overly strict, parent. I grew up with the stories of you all in my ears. He told me all of them so often that I had dreams about them. My mother hated it. She hated that he told me stories, she hated the stories he told me. I think mostly she just hates me and I took up time that father could have spent with her. I feel certain that she loved him a lot once. He took me out hunting, let me run through the fields. He took me to meet our people as he went about what he considered to be his duties. I think, overall, he was a good man. Perhaps not the exciting or glamorous type my mother may have wished for, but a good man."

The king has been listening intently and I am a little nervous to have so much of his focus on me. He says, "You say what he considered to be his duties. What do you mean by that?"

I chuckle with memories, saying, "My father did a great many things for the people we were charged with caring for. If something broke, he went to them and made sure it was fixed. If someone had a hard year, he eased it by whatever means he could. He was always willing to lend a hand at the farms. One day, some other nobles were out riding and saw my father helping to repair a fence. They didn't recognize my father, and they laughed at the 'peasants', telling them that they would tell my father how they were letting his lands fall to ruin." I laugh as I remember what happened next, telling him, "My father was so mad that he pulled Judda down from his horse, letting him land in the dirt. He told him that he had better never hear of him speaking so rudely to his people. Judda offered some excuse about not recognizing him, and that just made it worse. My father told him it didn't matter whether or not he was there. Judda made fun of him for getting dirty with the 'peasants'. And he told Judda that if he and his friend didn't leave now, he would tell his wife about all three of his mistresses and how much money he spent on them."

King Knox laughed loudly, saying, "Oh, I think I would have liked your father a great deal. How did he know about Judda's proclivities?"

"I asked him a similar question when we were alone on the way home. He said that he found a long time ago that most of the other nobles forgot where they came from and that they would not be accepting his ways any time soon. Because of that, he knew they would be his enemies sooner or later, so he was proactive. He hired people to keep tabs on each of them and just report on all the things they did. He said that he knew the neighbors' finances better than they did."

King Knox chuckles, saying, "Your father seems a crafty man. So, many of the nobles do not remember where they came from? My brothers and I may have stepped back too far for too long. But that is a worry for another day. What happened when you went to Ingemar's home for help?"

I look away, telling him, "King Knox, you don't really want to know that? It is nothing and will be easily resolved once I have secured my estates."

He stops us in the middle of the walkway, his hand coming to my chin and forcing me to look at him. "You may call me Knox and I assure you," he growls, "I very much want to know every detail of what happened at Ingemar's home."

The intensity of him should frighten me. By the way, his eyes are reflecting the light of the moon. The deep growl that accompanied those words should terrify me. Instead, every fiber of my being wants to press closer to the beast within him. The scent of him fills my very being and my hand tightens on his arm as a new flood of liquid fire erupts in my core. His nostrils flare and suddenly the arm that was under my hand is around my waist, lifting me as his face gets closer to mine. His eyes flash when I put my hands on his shoulders and he presses my body to his, the hand on my chin moving to tangle in my hair as his lips press against mine. A shock of electricity zaps me as his lips move against mine and it sets me free from the stupor his delicious scent had me trapped in. My lips open to him and he takes my mouth with his, its more of a fierce possession than a kiss. My fingers curl into his shoulders as I work to keep up with the inferno that is his kiss.

He breaks the kiss, leaving me to gasp for air as he kisses a trail of fire down my neck. I have brief thoughts of what if he bites me but quickly decide I don't care, this feels too good. His teeth nip at my neck, sending lightning racing through my body, a moan escaping my lips. Then he freezes, cocking his head to one side before he presses a last kiss on my neck and sets me down. I am confused and a little annoyed that he stopped when I hear the footsteps. Understanding dawns and I release his shoulders, running my fingers through my hair and straightening my clothes. He does the same and by the time the steps reach us; we are looking at a lovely statue hidden in the foliage.

Eight

K nox

* * *

Epaphras has the worst possible timing. By the time he arrives, I am showing Valdís a statue of a wolf, hidden off to the side of this part of the garden. Epaphras spots me and says, "Sire, we have a little bit of a problem. V—" He stops as I turn and he catches sight of her on my other side, "Oh. I see. She is with you. Well, very good then. I will just go. Have a lovely evening. Do let me know if you need anything at all."

I nod as I watch him turn and walk as fast as he can while still maintaining his decorum. I chuckle and look down at Valdís, "Come, my little escapee, let us walk the gardens before we do any other dangerous things."

She nods, her lips still swollen from our kiss and her pulse wild. Focus. Show her the damn rose garden. We begin to walk, her hand back on my arm. It feels so right to have her here with me, but it can't be. She can't be the one from the story her father wouldn't have known to be able to tell her. It just isn't possible. The roses are in full bloom, which is odd, they weren't last night.

We have several gardens and as I stroll through them with her; I press her for more information. I learn her father told her each of the tales many times, but as I knew he couldn't have, he didn't tell her the story of our mate. She can recite the blessing from memory. Her mother has never liked her, and she is likely to be problematic if anyone finds out that I kissed Valdís before I made my decree. My brothers will support me either way. And Valdís is only concerned that her people remain well cared for. I can achieve that without letting either of them have it, if I need to resort to that. She is so turned on in my presence and the scent of her is driving me to distraction. I want to fuck her here in the garden.

I fear I will be lost in her if I do. She can smell the pheromones. The Goddess said that we would begin to exude pheromones when she had been born and that, to the right woman, it would be intoxicating. But Valdís can't be who we have been waiting for all this time. She is only seventy; she hasn't even made her first one hundred. Surely the Goddess wouldn't want us to take one so young into this life of blood and violence and the demands of ruling? Or did she? Perhaps I underestimate Valdís? "Tell me about you?"

She laughs, and it is music to my ears as she says, "I have been talking this entire time. Aren't you tired of listening to me prattle on? Besides, you have lived so much longer than I, and you were not restricted to your home unless out with your father. I imagine your stories are so much better."

I laugh at how neatly she turned that around on me, telling her, "You wouldn't deny your king a request, would you?"

"Oh, King Knox," she starts, and I cut her off.

"I asked you to call me Knox."

"Hmm, actually you told me to call you Knox." a shiver runs down my spine when she says my name. "I can let that slide. However, I am fresh out of stories for you. You are going to have to reveal stories about yourself or find another way to carry the conversation, Knox."

"So the kitten has more than just an ability to land on her feet and a body made of curves and valleys that drive a man to distraction?"

She looks up at me, asking, "You find my body distracting?"

"Very. Your scent too. You smell like a sweets shop and I find a sudden desire for dessert."

Her breath catches, and the scent of her honey hits the air again. I can't take it. And I spin her to face me as my arms go round her, pulling her body against mine. I know she can feel what she is doing to me. How her scent, her body, and that mind are affecting me. Her hands are against my chest and she runs them up my shoulders to my neck and lightly scratches. A shudder runs through my body as her questing fingers find my hair and she tugs lightly. I know I shouldn't be holding this little mortal against my body. And I definitely shouldn't be kissing her, but I find my hands have cupped her sweet, round ass and I'm sliding her body up my own till her succulent lips are within reach. I take her mouth as mine, my tongue invading her the way my cock is desperate to do. Her hands curl into little fists in my hair as she gives as good as she is getting. Her legs swing out and wrap themselves around my waist. I can feel the heat of her core through the fabric of our clothing. She moans into me when I thrust up with my hips, pressing my cock against her.

Oh Goddess, her kisses are fire in my veins. She breaks the kiss, gasping for air even as she kisses her way down my neck to bite me. I nearly come right there. I press her body down on my cock and my teeth descend. She bites me again and squeezes with her legs. A moan escapes me. Oh Goddess, no one else has ever had enough access to bite me and fuck, I need her to do it more. Then she freezes in my arms, her body stiff for a moment before she swings her legs down and whispers, "Put me down, Knox. We can't do this. You still have to rule on my petition and I have an entire battle when I go home, even if you side with me. I'll still have to make mother and those loyal to her leave. I can't ask more of you." She taps my shoulder like I didn't hear everything she said. "Knox! Put me down!"

I look down at her, her eyes widen slightly at the sight of my fangs, but she still kicks her legs in an attempt to gain my cooperation in setting her down. I press her body closer to mine. She moans and her head drops a little as my cock digs into her soft flesh. With a sigh, I ease her down my body, causing more friction. It feels so good, but I release her when her feet are steady on the ground. She busies herself with righting her shirt before she looks up and says, "Thank you." Then she tips her head to one side, asking, "Do they hurt?"

I am confused at first. Is she asking about my balls? Then I remember my teeth, saying, "Oh," I bring a hand up to touch one, "these? No. They haven't hurt in a long time. But that is maybe just because I have had them so long." She watches in fascination as my teeth retract. I allow it, even as I realize I need to send her away. I can't have her here when my brother arrives. Who am I kidding? I can't have her here with me. As I guide her back toward the castle, I resolve that I will have her sent to one of the seaside castles. She will enjoy it there while we investigate, and she won't be here to distract me. Yes. That will work just about perfect. And if she leaves tomorrow, I won't have time to become further attached to her.

Managing not to kiss her again or take her into her room was an act of willpower. This is why she has to go away. I pass one of my employees and ask them to please send Epaphras to me. They take off at a run and I shake my head. I must look frightening again. Great.

I haven't made it much farther when Epaphras comes running up, "You requested me, sire?"

"I did. You didn't need to run, though. I want her sent to one of the seaside castles while we investigate this."

He blanches, "What? But you seemed to be getting along so well? I thought maybe..."

Shrugging, I tell him, "That just isn't meant to be for

any of us. She is a temptation that I don't need. She may have the run of the castle by the sea, and I want you to send two men to keep her safe. Get all that prepped so she can leave after her breakfast in the morning." And that will give me time to see her once more before she is gone from my life. "Once she has gone, I think we will pay her mother a visit. As well as Ingemar. We will be blissfully free of paperwork for the whole day."

Valdís

* * *

Epaphras came to get me early this morning for breakfast. I was barely awake when he burst in, talking a mile a minute about my need to pack. I reminded him that I own a total of two outfits here. Packing is pretty quick. He rolled his eyes at me. But after that he left the room, telling me to get dressed and he would be back shortly. When he shut the door behind himself I jumped out of bed and threw on the clothes I arrived in. Luckily, the castle employees had washed them, because I do not know where to do that here.

He came back quickly as promised and now I am out on a veranda facing the gardens, a breakfast of fruits, eggs, and crepes before me. The tea is mostly what I am focused on for the moment. I feel like something big is coming today. I can't tell if I should be afraid or excited.

I am picking at the fruit when I feel his eyes on me. I can't say how I know it is him watching me, but I do.

Looking around but I don't see him. Kings. Fine. If he doesn't want to be seen, that's his choice. I hear a rustling in the bushes off to my left. Do they have animals here? He can't be hiding in the bushes? No, it has to be a creature of some sort. Maybe a cat?

I pick up a berry, these really are delicious. There is that rustling again. I wonder if the cat will come out if I call it? I look over to call the kitty out of the bushes just in time to see a man burst out of them at me. Before I can scream, he hits my head with something and darkness takes over my world.

Nine

K nox

* * *

I watch her as Epaphras settles her on the veranda. She is really lovely. Her dark hair hanging down her back. I want to keep her here, but if I do that. If I did that, she wouldn't be safe. Even from here, I want to bite her. Mark her. Make her my own. But I can't. She isn't the one from the stories. Every woman any of us ever tried to have a relationship with, every woman that we tried to love, every one of them died by our own hands. I won't do that to another innocent woman, not again. No one should die for the crime of being loved by me.

I watch as she turns her head, scanning the perimeter. I wonder if she feels my presence? Why is she paying attention to the bushes over there? I step closer to the one-way glass that is allowing me to observe her undetected. I don't see anything, maybe some infinitesimal movement, but that could be the wind.

Watching her without going to her is causing an ache that I don't understand. She isn't the one. It isn't possible. She is just another one that I have been drawn to over the years. I'm not going to fuck up her life just for a small taste of happy in mine. I am so caught up watching her that I don't see the men until one hits her with a small club. A roar rips from my throat as she drops to the pavement. I race to the veranda, arriving just as one of them puts her over his shoulder. I hit him and pull her to me before he falls. Laying her down on the paving stones, because her blood is singing, it's calling for me to drink. I run to catch the other man and bring him back to the veranda. Taking away all his weapons, I knock him out, too. One clean hit and I just drop him to the paving stones. I can hear people in the castle running out here as I lift her gently from where she lays. The blood coming from the wound on her head is insanely tempting. I have never wanted anyone's blood so much. Usually our people's blood is mostly repellant to us. Trying to drink from them would make us want to vomit if we took more than a little.

But her blood, oh goddess, I want it so much. My fangs drop, slicing my own lips as they descend. The taste of my blood does nothing to satisfy me, but it does drip onto her. Epaphras arrives at a run as I am walking in the doorway with two guards behind him. I tell the guards, "Fetch those bodies and put them in cages. I'll deal with them later when they wake up. Epaphras, fetch the doctor. I am taking her to the blue study."

. . .

Valdís

* * *

My head hurts so damn much. Why? The memories of what happened just before everything went black slam into place and I try to sit up, hands push me down and two voices tell me to stay still. The pounding in my head agrees with them, so I lay back. I recognize one of the voices, and ask, "Epaphras, what happened? Why did that guy hit me? Was he an over-zealous guard or something?"

Epaphras hisses, "Our guards would never! Put that thought out of your mind. It appears that someone scaled the walls and intended to kidnap you. Luckily, our king got you before they got anywhere."

The other voice tells me, "Could you open your eyes for me, Valdís? I would like to see how they are focusing."

Keeping my eyes stubbornly shut, I ask him, "Are you planning to shine a bright light in my eyes? Because my head is pounding and that feels like it would hurt."

He chuckles and I hear a growl in the room. I frown as he says, "I will refrain from shining any lights in your eyes until you are ready to consent to it."

Satisfied, I crack my eyes just a tiny bit. I see two blurry, vaguely human shapes before me. One standing and the other kneeling to peer at me. The light isn't terribly bright in here and my brains aren't hurting more with this amount of light, so I go ahead and fully open them. It takes just a second for them to focus, and I see a strange man kneeling next to me and staring intently at my eyes while Epaphras hovers over him. I search for the source of the growl and I see the king across the room pacing, his fangs out and blood on his shirt. "Are you okay, Knox?"

He looks over at me, brows raised and mouth hanging open, "Are you kidding? I'm fine! You are the one that was injured. Pay attention to the doctor and do what he says. Don't worry about me!"

"You don't have to snap at me. It's not like I got hurt intentionally!"

Epaphras interjects, "Perhaps we could check your eyes now? Are you feeling well enough for that?"

I focus on him and the doctor, "I suppose. Is there anything we can do for this pain? My head is pounding."

The doctor nods, saying, "We can give you some painkillers as soon as I finish the examination. How do you feel about injections?"

"They aren't my favorite, but I can live with it if it means that my head stops pounding."

"Ok," he holds up his little flashlight, "this is going to be bright. But I need to see how your eyes react to the stimuli before I can give you anything." He shines the light in my eyes and it isn't the most pleasant thing ever, but he nods and mumbles things. I watch as he reaches into his bag and pulls out a syringe and a bottle. He loads the syringe and looks at me, asking, "Ass or arm?"

Knox growls from across the room. I look over, "You have got to be kidding. Any more of that and I will show him my whole ass. What are you on about? Here doc, I need all my brain power, stab me in the arm. Maybe it will make it to my brain faster that way."

Knox growls out, "Can we get her something else to wear? Get the blood cleaned up off of her?"

Epaphras shoots a look at the king that I don't understand, as he says, "Yes. I'll send someone to find her something to wear." He goes to the door and has a hushed conversation with someone before going to the king and whispering to him. That's not suspicious at all. The doctor is cleaning my head and telling me he doesn't think I will need stitches, but I should definitely try to rest a little more. I tell him I will, knowing that is absolutely a lie. The doctor's face says he knows I am lying too, but he is too polite to call me on it. Someone knocks on the door and Epaphras answers it, coming away with a stack of clothing for me. He hands them to me as the doctor moves away, then stands there watching me expectantly. I know he doesn't expect I am going to change in front of everyone.

I sit up slowly, the pounding in my head is easing already. Looking Epaphras in the eyes, I tell him, "I will not be changing clothes in a roomful of men. Are you high or something?"

He has the grace to blush, and Knox looks up from his conversation with the doctor.

Knox tells them, "Get out. I will stay and make sure she remains safe."

Epaphras looks at me and shrugs before he leaves the room. I stand slowly and tell Knox, "You are not staying in here while I change! I don't care if we kissed. You don't get to see me naked."

Knox stalks his way over to me, leaning down to look me in the eye, "Listen carefully, little snack, I am staying here. They were trying to kidnap you from my castle. You will stay here until I can figure out why they want you so bad. I was planning to turn my back on you while you change, but if you are going to fight me about it, I will change your clothes myself."

"You wouldn't!"

"I fucking would." He turns his back to me, saying, "Now change your clothes before I do."

The bastard. He probably would too. I hurriedly strip off my blood-soaked clothing and put on the stretchy clothing they brought for me. It doesn't leave much to the imagination, but it is something. He turns around the minute I have everything in place and I just know he has been focused on the sounds of my dressing the entire time. I find myself turned on by the idea that someone wants me enough to pay attention so closely. I watch his nostrils flare and his hands clench into fists as he says, "I don't know what you are thinking, but it would be great if you could think about something else."

I grin. So this makes him uncomfortable? Great. "I was thinking about how closely you must have been paying attention to the sounds of clothing on my skin. It was kind of hot knowing that someone was paying that much attention to me."

His eyes flash and he clenches his jaw so hard I wonder if vampires can break their teeth. Then he leans in and picks me up, knees across one arm and back against the other, and

I shout, "What in the fuck do you think you are doing? Put me down!"

He just laughs, saying, "I am the king. I can carry you if I want. Deal with it." He carries me to the door, ordering me to, "Open the door." I turn the knob and pull it open. He steps back as I do. I let go, allowing it to finish swinging open. As he carries me through the castle, he tells me, "I need you to see if you recognize the men that tried to kidnap you. But they are in the dungeon. The doctor said you need rest, not exertion. I am going to carry you down there and back up after you identify them. The sooner you accept that, the easier this will be for you."

"You have them? I hope I don't recognize them." I turn my face away as he carries me. It already hurts to think about what it means if I recognize them. All too quickly, we are in the dungeon and the guards are escorting us to a row of cells. They stop in front of one and Knox stops too, turning to face one of the cages. I look into the cage and I see my mother's guard, Henson.

Tears slipping down my face unchecked, I ask him, "Was it you that hit me, Henson?" He shakes his head no, and Knox turns us to face the cell across from Henson. I peer into that one. It is darker, but I finally see the shape of a man sitting in the back right corner. "It's too dark in there and too bright out here for me to see him." A guard reaches into the cell and flips a switch. I see his clothing and that brown hair, saying, "Oh Michael, how could you? You hit me?" He keeps his face down, refusing to look at me.

I guess Knox heard enough as he turns and starts walking away from the cages. As he walks, I hear Michael call out, anguish in his voice, "I'm sorry! I'm so sorry." My heart can't take anymore of this terrible day.

As he carries me back through the maze of the castle, Knox asks me, "Who are they? How do you know them?"

Continuing to look down, I answer him, "They are guards in my mother's employ. I thought... It doesn't matter what I thought."

"Tell me what you thought, please."

Fresh tears burning my eyes, I tell him, "I thought they were my friends. They were my father's guards for a long time. I just, I don't understand how they could go along with this. Actually move to carry it out. Michael actually hit me with something that knocked me out. I thought, I thought that because they had seemed to be my friends, that would remain as I came here to try to get help. But it looks like I was wrong."

Knox squeezes me into his broad chest, his chin coming to rest on my head. The tears continue to fall as he walks. When he stops, we are in front of a door I don't recognize, and the guard opens it for him before backing out of the way. It appears to be a bedroom? "Why didn't you take me to the room I have been staying in? Did they try to get in there too?"

He sets me down on the softest thing I have ever set my ass upon and kneels before me. "I brought you to my quarters because I need you to be somewhere safe while I handle things. This room is one of the safest in the entire castle. And it is very unlikely that anyone would think to look for you here based on my reputation. You are the only woman that has been inside this room in centuries. Women are not generally allowed in this wing at all. Relax, rest, and if you choose to do so, you are welcome to read anything you like in my book collection." He gestures toward a wall of shelves filled with books. "Epaphras will bring you food very shortly." He produces a small knife from somewhere, saying, "if anyone strange does come in here, stab them with this until I arrive."

"You want me to stab someone?"

"No, I want you to continually stab them until I arrive. Scream too. Most people will not believe you would fight back and even fewer will be capable of doing much to you as long as you perforate them properly."

"Perforate? Oh my goddess, I am never going to look at that word the same again."

Ten

nox

* * *

Epaphras is waiting when I step outside my suite. Ignoring him to turn and tell the guards stationed at either side of the door, I tell them, "If anyone or anything gets in there and injures her even the slightest, your lives will be forfeit. Keep her safe."

Both guards nod and manage to keep their incredulity to a minimum. Starting down the hall with Epaphras hot on my heels, I tell him, "Fine. She stays. We need more guards for her specifically. I want her to have the best. She balks even at stabbing people."

"Sire, tell me you didn't ask her to stab anyone?"

"I don't lie Epaphras. Though what I actually told her was to keep stabbing someone until I could get there. And considering she was attacked on the veranda this morning, it isn't unreasonable to assume that she is likely to be attacked again. With the exception of right now, she is to be kept away from our wing. Beyond that, give her the run of the castle. At least one guard with her at all times while inside the castle, on the grounds two."

Noticing that Epaphras is struggling to keep up, I slow till he is able to walk even with me. Once he has caught his breath, he says, "How long do we intend to keep her here? Will Malic need to be made aware of her? Are you still leaving when he arrives?"

I stop mid step. A few days. I am supposed to leave in a few days. Shit. That's not happening. "When is my brother due?"

"Sometime in the next few days, depending on the weather."

"I see. Yes. Let him know the current situation in full and that I will still be here when he arrives. It is likely that I will stay until this is resolved. He should know that, too."

"It will be done. Sire, I know you hate them, but there is a petition waiting for your attention that I think you will want to take care of immediately."

"Fuck Epaphras, today of all days? Really?"

"Well, I think this will help to work on some of those things. Really, sire, you will want to take care of this one now. Though there are a few others that won't take long."

Why would he be so insistent? "Who is petitioning us?"

Knox

* * *

Epaphras said he didn't want to spoil the surprise but that I would immediately understand as soon as I saw them. So I decide on the third petition of the day and watch as they leave. One couple was disgruntled because they couldn't take over a part of their neighbor's property and the other couple was cautiously optimistic. I make a note to have Epaphras check on the one couple in two weeks to ensure the other couple is following my judgement.

The next set of people walk in, they look familiar. It can't be. Did they really come here to petition? This should be good. As they stop before me, I ask, "What issue is it you are here to have solved?"

Eirene speaks first, which appears to annoy Ingemar. She says, "I seek the return of my dearest daughter. She is my eldest child and is really not well. I was told she had been seen going to the castle. I pray you will return her safe."

"Tell me more about how she is unwell." Is she really smiling and batting her eyes at me? "Do you have something in your eye? I can have a bucket of water fetched to fix that."

Ingemar seems entertained by the idea, but Eirene is not as she responds, "If I must. We have worked hard to keep our shame a secret. My Valdís has never been right. Her mind is broken. She sees things that aren't there, believes everyone is out to get her. She has this entire delusion that I hate her! I could never hate my darling first born. She is the light of my life, even on the bad days."

I nod, "I see. And why is Ingemar here?"

Ingemar takes the opportunity to speak before Eirene, his face triumphant. Are they not aware of their facial expressions? "Sire, though we seek for Valdís to be released into Eirene's custody, she is to marry my son very soon. As we are nearly family and Eirene has so recently lost her husband, I offered to come for support. My son is keen to marry his bride and start his life as husband and father."

I will kill Ingemar's son myself before I let him marry Valdís.

Eirene picks up where Ingemar left off, saying, "Exactly. My daughter should be home with her family during her last days as a maiden. Before she becomes the wife of dear Pelos, who has agreed to take her on knowing that she will never be a proper life partner and all the responsibility will lie on his shoulders. Incidentally, we sent some of our men to find her and they seem to be missing? Do you perhaps have them in your care as well?"

These people. "I do. I have both your daughter and your men in my care, as you put it."

A sly look crosses Eirene's face so quickly a regular human wouldn't have noticed. Just as quickly, she is crying and shouting, "OH! Thank the Goddess my sweet girl is safe! My guards are safe!"

She just repeats herself over and over. I wait for her to stop and tell her, "I didn't say they were all safe."

The shock on her face is priceless as she demands things from me, shrieking, "You will give me my daughter and my guards! How dare you keep them prisoner here! What kind of monster are you to hold a young woman with a broken mind hostage like this? For shame! Outside of the safety of her family, I have to wonder what you have been doing, keeping a young woman in her condition here against her will!"

Ingemar interjects, saying, "I feel the need to inform you that my son will sue for the damage done to his wife during her captivity here, and everyone will know what kind of monster you really are."

They are so ridiculous that I can't help but to laugh. They fall silent, watching me laugh at them. Their fear stench fills the room as I look at them, letting a little of the monster I really am show. When I let my laughter die, they are both staring at me with mouths hanging open. I tell them, "Your men will be held pending the investigation into the attempted kidnapping of one of my guests is completed. My guest, your daughter Eirene, will remain my guest for the time being. She is part of the investigation. As the two of you are so fully invested in the guards and Valdís, perhaps you would like to join the guards in their spacious dungeon accommodations? Then you would be kept fully aware of how the investigation is progressing."

They both blanch and Eirene says, "That will not be necessary, your majesty, though your offer is more than generous. We have the utmost faith that your decree will be in everyone's best interest. We will happily go home and await your commands there. Each of us has much to do this time of year, myself especially as this is the first year of Conrí's passing and I am finding out how many things I took for granted because he was so good at them. I'm sure you understand."

I chuckle and watch them flinch, before I tell them, "Indeed. I do understand. You may both leave now."

I watch as they all but run from the throne room. Epaphras steps up to my left side. I turn to him, saying, "Have some of our spies follow them. Watch and investigate."

He bows, "It will be done." Then turns and leaves the throne room. Hiring that man was possibly the best decision we ever made.

Eirene

* * *

"That infernal man!"

Ingemar looks crossly at me, saying, "Perhaps you could wait till we are in the car before starting this tirade? Somewhere that the king will not get word of everything you say?"

I scowl at him but fall silent. We make it to the car and as soon as the doors are closed, I explode into a rant, "How dare he keep my daughter and my people? I can't believe he would do that! And he threatened me! What kind of king goes around threatening his people?"

Ingemar sits with his arms crossed over his chest while I rant. Once I finish, he says, "Perhaps we can work this to our advantage? What if we begin a smear campaign against them? I mean, I doubt very seriously the Goddess is still around, she certainly isn't answering prayers. So it stands to reason, they don't have their backer either. We can use this to spread rumors to the rest of the island. Perhaps we can take the throne. Then we could make some real changes."

It annoys me that he thought of this first. He isn't wrong, but I should have thought of this first. Now he can say it was all his idea. I refrain from smiling, as I recall how often healthy men have accidents. Better if he doesn't think about these things. "You're absolutely right. We need to start rumors about it all. Tell everyone that will listen about King Knox holding my dear daughter hostage, how she isn't well and should be with her family. How this is delaying the wedding. Your son should act sad and tell people in passing as well. As I think about this, the king seems keen to investigate. I may need to tie up some loose ends at my house. What about yours? Are there any unhappy souls there just looking for an excuse?"

He appears to be thinking as he looks out the window, so I wait. Patience always serves me well. I am rewarded when he turns to me, saying, "I think not, but I will be watchful just in case. You said you have some loose ends to tie up?"

"Hm, yes. Several. There are a few servants that have been steadfast in their loyalty to my daughter. I think they will go on an extended vacation."

He smiles as the car pulls up to his door, saying, "And will those servants ever return from their vacations?"

"Of course not. They needed to go anyway. This is just a good time for it. I think we should station people around the castle to monitor her. We need to know if he tries to sneak her off to another castle or something."

He nods as he gets out of the car, turning back to say, "Agreed. I will send some men up there. Some that will take the opportunity to collect her if one should arise."

"Fantastic. I'll see you soon."

When I arrive home, I tell my guards to round up everyone loyal to Valdís. They take off and I head for my dead husband's office. I am making myself a drink when the guard comes to tell me, "We can't find them, mistress."

"What do you mean you can't find them? They can't have just disappeared."

"They did, Mistress. Their rooms are empty and they don't appear to be on the property at all."

"Fuck this day. Ok, go see if you can find them. If you can't find them, bring back some of their family. They'll come running back for them. Go!"

I watch them scramble to follow my orders as I take a sip of my drink. We have to get them under my control before the king's investigation gets this far.

Ingemar

* * *

The widow Eirene is definitely up to something. Her face was all too calm for that entire conversation. I feel certain she will double cross me at the first opportunity. After all, I plan to do the same for her. Hulthen falls in behind me as I walk to my office. While I get seated, he prepares a drink for me and sets it on the desk before standing opposite me to await his orders. He has been such a dutiful servant.

I take a sip of my drink. It is just the way I like it. "Very good Hulthen. Now, I need a group of men to go up to the castle unseen and watch. They are to watch for Valdís, and if they see an opportunity, collect her and bring her quickly away from the castle. Who do you think would fit the bill?"

"I can think of four immediately, possibly a couple more when I check further."

"Excellent. Find them and get them dispatched now."

Eleven

V aldís

* * *

Knox left me to rot in his room for most of the day. They brought my lunch in here. Now these stuffy guards that won't even tell me their names are here to escort me to my quarters. Ugh. They do tell me that Epaphras plans to see me in my quarters and tell me more about what is planned for me. I guess that will have to do.

I follow the lead guard and I kind of feel like I am in a parade. A small parade, but a parade. We make it to my quarters without incident. I would have been more surprised if there was an incident. Epaphras is waiting in the sitting area of my room when I arrive. I shut the door on my new guards stationed in the hall and ask him, "What is going on? Why did he leave me cooped up in his suite all day?"

Epaphras chuckles, "I will get to that. But first, the king has made some decisions regarding you. You will be given free rein of the castle with the exception of the king's wing. They prefer that to be a private space and he asks that you respect that." I nod my agreement because really, that is fair. Epaphras continues, "The other caveat is that at least one guard goes with you everywhere inside the castle. If you decide to step out of the castle, it is to be a minimum of two. I want to say here, that if you give the guards a hard time and ditch them or something, they will be punished. The guards here are good people and the king is trying to ensure your safety. That being said, I would appreciate it if you do not get my friends punished."

"I understand Epaphras. And I will behave in that respect. I don't really want people in trouble on my behalf anyway. Is that all? Will you tell me what else is going on now?"

He nods, and proceeds to tell me all about my Mother's and Ingemar's petition today. "Those bastards! I have never been mentally ill! Why would they say that? That is horrible, to falsely accuse someone of things that people actually have to deal with? I never dreamed either of them could be so awful. Well, I might have dreamed my mother could be so awful. I am still surprised at the depths they have sunk to."

"If it helps, the king sent them back home after offering to let them await the conclusion of his investigation in the dungeon with the two guards already in there."

My jaw drops as I say, "Oh no! Really? Mother is definitely irate. Who knows what she will do over this? Knox should probably watch his back."

He stands, "Perhaps, but for now, we will provide you with a wardrobe as you certainly cannot go home and get your clothing. Goddess knows you would be snatched up and married off to that odious boy of Ingemar's. Now stand up and let's get your measurements." He pulls out a measuring tape from somewhere as I stand. Those pants are very fitted. Where was he hiding it? The thought passes as he measures every inch of my body. For some reason, it didn't occur to me that he would be so very thorough. He is fast, and it is over before I can get more than surprised.

"Now that I have those, I'll be going to tend to this. If you need anything, you can let the guards at the door know or wander out to find someone yourself. Have a lovely evening. A tray should be here for dinner shortly."

My dinner arrived, and I devoured it. Nervous energy had me pacing a large part of the day. Rest be damned. After pacing my room for a solid hour, I decide to wander the castle. I open the door and two very big men turn to look at me from either side of the door. "I want to wander the castle. Epaphras said I could as long as I let you all come with me. Aren't you bored standing here?"

The two look at each other, shrug, and turn back to nod at me. I step through the two of them and one reaches behind me, shutting the door. Walking down the hall toward the main area of the castle, I ask the guards what their favorite rooms are in this place. They remain silent, gargoyles creeping along behind me. The castle is huge, and moving from one room to another is ridiculous. Why is everything so far apart? The library is magnificent, and I spent some time perusing the variety in there. Focus is not my strong point right now, so I leave the library without a book.

The game room is boring with only the two gargoyles behind me for company, and they refuse to play a game with me. Eventually I smell food. Maybe the kitchen staff will talk to me? Following my nose, I make it to the kitchen. I peek in and say, "Hi, is it ok to come in?"

The cook jumps and spins to look at me with a scowl ready on his face, a finger coming up to wag. He sees me and his eyes round, his lips spreading into a wide smile, as he says, "Valdís! Come in! Come in!" I step in and he crosses the room in a flash, arms around me in greeting, before he pulls back and puts his hands on my shoulders, saying, "You probably don't know about me, but I know a great deal about you. I am so glad you are here. My cousin will be so glad to hear that you are well!"

"What? Who is your cousin?"

"Why, she really never did tell you. I thought she must have been joking all this time. Dagma is my cousin. My favorite cousin. Our mothers are still neighbors. We talk often."

"Dagma? My Dagma? You are her cousin? No way! She told me about her cousin, but she never mentioned you were here!" We embrace once more before he leads me to a table and has me sit in one of the chairs.

"Let me get you some food. Would you like some

tea?" He didn't wait for me to answer as he turned and set to doing just that. "Dagma told me over the years about your mother. It's a shame, mother being so awful to her daughter. I'll never understand it. Dagma has never understood it. But she has been telling me all these years about the awful. I know King Knox will do right by you, so I was mightily relieved when you showed up here. Imagine the sheer audacity to try to kidnap you from here!"

"It was wild. I feel bad for the guys sitting in the dungeon now. They are her victims too. But I think it will all work out. King Knox says he is doing an investigation."

"Excellent! If he wants to hear the stories Dagma has been telling me all these years, you let him know I am happy to rat that horrible woman out. Some of the things that Dagma told me would curl a person's toes! It's funny how people people rarely notice the workers around them. Dagma told me things that even you don't know about. They would just horrify you. It's all right though, our Dagma, she's been writing me letters all this time. One of your guards can fetch them from the nightstand in my quarters right now. Those will provide all the evidence his highness could need."

I look to my guards but they are already on top of it and one is leaving the kitchen even as I look. The one that stayed behind nods and lifts one side of his mouth in what I think was meant to be a smile.

Cook carries on telling me about the castle and the people in it as he is making my food. About halfway through, I realize none of the people he has been telling me about are women. I wait till he pauses to ask, "Are there no women in the castle?"

He says, "Not a one. The kings got so sick of the women that wanted to be queen trying to marry them or be caught in a compromising position with them that they just banned them entirely from the castle."

"What? That is ridiculous. Who would want to be queen? My father taught me about running our estates, and that is a lot of work. I can't imagine being queen would be less work, especially over all? Fuck that."

Cook chuckles as he brings a plate and glass to me, saying, "I don't think they intended to do any of the work, they just wanted the power."

"Well, that is just awful. No wonder the kings don't want any women in here. I guess that explains why none of them are married either. I kind of feel sorry for them. Trapped into an existence where all they are is glorified protectors for the people here. No friends or love, just an eternity of duty. And blood. It seems like a lonely, depressing life. I can understand why they spend so much of it sleeping."

The plate he set before me looks so good and I dig in. It is as delicious as it looks. The glass is something fruity, tasty and completely divine. We talk about Dagma and he tells me stories from their childhood that have me laughing and trying not to spew this delicious food all over him when Epaphras and the other guard enter the kitchen. Epaphras walks directly to the cook holding up a stack of letters, asking, "Is this all of them? Do you have more at home?"

"No, I don't go there enough to keep them secure. So I

just kept them all here in case they were needed one day. My cousin was afraid that something would happen to this one," he gestures at me, "and she wanted people to know it wasn't an accident if it did happen. Because she was afraid that something would happen to her too."

"And I left her there. I promised I would come back. Oh sweet Goddess, I hope she left when she found out I wasn't able to get back that night. I told her she had to leave if I wasn't there before I was missed. Have you heard from her today? Or yesterday?"

"The last letter on the pile came in today. It said she and the others loyal to you would be out of there by the time this reached me, but she wouldn't say where in case it was intercepted. I have ideas, but it would take me a day or so to find her if I needed to see her or my mother."

Epaphras looks as confused as I feel, so Cook says, "She took our mothers with her. She always said that if something happened, and she had to run, we would all have to hide. After I started working here, she told me I should stay here if she disappeared with our mothers, because that woman would be after us. Valdís, I'm sorry to be talking about your mother like this in front of you, but it's the honest truth. "

"I understand better than you think. My mother is not a good person. I would have to be a fool to not have noticed that in all this time. Really, she has never cared for my presence and has always been cruel to me. A good person isn't cruel to their own child. I faced the truth about her a long time ago." I let my eyes focus on the floor. Seeing the pity in their eyes isn't something I want to do today. Or any day, really. I know the kind of person my mother is. I've known since I was little and still desperately wished that somewhere was a mother that would love me the way I had seen other mothers love their children. But no where in my being did I ever harbor the idea that my mother would suddenly become a good person and care for me. That has always been outside the realm of possibility in my world.

I realize they have been speaking while I was lost in my thoughts and I tune in to hear Epaphras saying that he would be taking those letters to the king now. He asks my guard to walk with him, and when he looks unsure about leaving me again, I tell them, "Don't worry. I will stay here with your friend and Cook, all well behaved, till you get back." They leave quickly and I look at Cook, saying, "Tell me some more stories about when you and Dagma were little, please."

By the time the other guard got back, I was exhausted and ready to go back to my rooms. Sleep claimed me as soon as my head touched the pillow, which is why I screamed when Knox burst into my rooms and flipped on the lights without so much as a knock.

He clapped his hands over his ears till I was silent and then said, "Is that really necessary?"

This annoyed me greatly, probably because he just woke me up but the sass in me was the first to grab the wheel, "Was it necessary to burst into the room where I was sleeping and flip on a light as the door slammed closed behind you? Because most people fucking knock."

"I'm the king. Nobody cares about that. At least, not to my face."

"I am going to scream every single time you do that to me. And if you continue to talk to me for too long now without getting to the point of why you felt you had to come bother me right this minute, I may decide to scream till you leave the room."

"You wouldn't," he says with his eyes narrowed.

"Try me, sir. I value my sleep, and you have taken me from it. Why are you here?"

He brandishes some papers as he paces my room, saying, "Why didn't you mention any of this? There is so much here. Why didn't you talk about how she treated you?"

My fuzzy, sleep-deprived brain registers the papers in his hand, and I realize those must be Dagma's letters. Rubbing my face with both hands for a tiny bit of wakefulness, I tell him, "It wasn't pertinent to what I came her to get help with. I needed help with ensuring the inheritance goes as my father intended so that I can keep our people happy and safe. My history had nothing to do with that."

Knox looks like his head might pop off and begin to orbit the planet. "Not pertinent? Not pertinent? Are you joking? She has a long history of cruelty, especially towards you. This matters," He strides across the room toward me, grabbing my arms and snatching me up to my knees so I am face to face with him, "You matter! How can you not see that? Nothing she did is ok, and you deserve so much better than any of this."

I am so stunned I don't know what to do, as he wraps

his arms around me and holds me close. But the closeness is really nice. It feels so safe here in his arms. I snuggle into him, my eyes drooping. Maybe he would let me sleep here? He smells so nice. Next thing I know, he is laying me back in the spot I had been sleeping in before he snatched me up. His face is tender as he covers me with a blanket, but my eyes are heavy and close, though I want to study the tender look and find out who it is for.

I wake again, and it is daylight. I can't help but wonder if last night was real. Did the king really bust into my room to ask me questions about things I didn't talk about to try to sway him to my cause because they had no bearing? I look around the room and I can't see even a trace of his having been here. "Valdís, you were obviously dreaming hard. Now go get yourself dressed and find some food before your belly eats a hole through your spine."

Dressing takes no time. Epaphras hung clothes in the closet in groups to be worn together. Since I am not overly concerned with what I wear, that works for me. Today is a pair of pants with loose legs that make it almost look like a skirt paired with a fitted top. Opening the door, I find a new set of guards. I didn't think it was possible for anyone to look more serious than the two from yesterday, but these have them beat. Sizing them up has me quickly deciding to skip the pointless questions and just search out the kitchen. I found my way there yesterday, I can do it again. I know Cook will welcome me in there. He'll talk to me too.

Fifteen minutes later, I am beginning to despair of ever

finding the kitchen before my attitude takes a serious turn and then that scent hits me. I am stopped, eyes closed and inhaling it when someone runs into me and I go flying toward the floor. Strong arms catch me and my eyes fly open to find Knox face to face with me. A rumble sounds in his chest and suddenly my panties are wet as I say, "You caught me."

He growls, "What shall I do with you now that I have?"

I might die of lust. This man, this king, is holding me up, our bodies pressed together so tight I can feel just how much he likes the contact, wants to know what to do with me now that he has caught me. I answer the only way an insanely horny woman can, "Whatever you would like to do."

He draws me closer and one of my gargoyles clears his throat. Knox's eyes flash and he straightens, pulling me with him. Once I am steadied on my feet, he asks, "Since we have so much company, where were you going?"

It takes me a moment to remember what I was looking for when I stopped, but I do, telling him, "The kitchen! I was looking for the kitchen. I need breakfast."

He extends an arm, saying, "Allow me to escort you." I slip my hand onto his arm and we head back the way he came. He murmurs, "Would you have dinner with me this evening?"

I glance up at him, telling him, "Yes, if you want me to?"

He looks over at me with a grin, saying, "Yes, I want you too."

I feel my face heating with a blush, and I turn to look at

the way before me. "Then I will have dinner with you tonight."

He stops before the door to the kitchen and says, "Very good. I can't stay to enjoy breakfast with you, as I have things to attend to, but I will see you this evening." Then he takes the hand that was on his arm and brings it to his lips, pressing a kiss on my knuckles. My entire body lights up and I can't help but wonder if there is something wrong with me. He smiles, a wicked gleam in his eyes as he leans in to whisper in my ear, "I love the reaction you have when I touch you. I look forward to finding out just how sensitive you are to my touch."

A shiver runs through my body and I moan a little. He leaves, going to do whatever he had planned for the day while I try to get myself together before I go in to see Cook. What is wrong with me? I have had sex before, been attracted to people many times, never have I been this affected by someone. A deep breath and I feel much more under control, instead of in heat.

Pushing through the kitchen door, I hear one of the gargoyles behind me chuckling and I let the door swing back on them instead of holding it open the way I normally would. I hear a very satisfying thud and "ooph!" I smile widely as I greet Cook.

Twelve

Valdís

* * *

I am a little terrified about dinner tonight. I don't know how I should act. Do I act like this is a date? I mean, he asked me to have dinner with him. But what if he just wants to tell me what he has decided and I show up dressed to seduce? Or what if he plans seduction and I show up dressed to hear a verdict? I cross the room, open the door and poke my head out, "Can one of you find Epaphras and ask him to come here, please? I really need him right now."

The left side gargoyle nods and sets off down the hall. I shout thank you at his back and close my door. I decide to tie the robe a little tighter and I can't find the ties. Looking down, I realize my robe was open when I spoke to the guards just now. I guess the good news in that is I had panties on? Closing the robe, I make damn sure I tie it this time, even tying the bow in case of the fabric having been at fault earlier because I would swear I tied it.

Epaphras knocks and opens the door just as I finish securing the robe. He tips his head at me and says, "I presume this is about dinner. Did you know your robe was open when you sent them for me? They appreciated the view either way."

Oh Goddess, they did see. Great. I watch him continue on toward the closet while I double check the security of the sash holding my robe closed, telling him, "Yes, I don't know how I should dress for this. I am not sure what the dinner is about. Is it about the hallway incident? Is it about my petition? Something else entirely?"

Epaphras looks back at me, saying, "The hallway incident?"

My face heats, "We ran, well, he ran into me when I stopped because of the scent I keep telling you about. And I think if one of my gargoyles hadn't cleared his throat we might have... you know, right there. In the hall. In front of everyone."

Epaphras laughs, "That happened this morning and you have doubts about what the dinner is about? My goodness, you have had sex before? Right?"

My eyes roll, "Yes! But I never had these kinds of reactions to anyone else. Never forgot there were other people in the hall with us. This kind of thing doesn't happen to me. Most of the people that wanted me were more interested in currying favor with my father by dating the one that was always with him. They didn't want me for me. Hell, I don't think they really wanted my body. They just liked that it was available. Most of them told me I would be cuter if I was smaller. Or if my waist were more trim. On and on with all their expectations. Mostly it amounts to I have too many curves to be with long term. I never forget who I am, where I am, or that I am not acceptable."

Epaphras sighs, "I see. May every one of those bastards suffer recurrent boils on their taints. I am not going to hug you right now, because I do not want the king to smell that I hugged you." He laughs ruefully, saying, "He is coming to some hard realizations, and he doesn't need that distraction. But I will say that you are worth so much more than those empty-headed idiots realized. Now, let's knock his socks off, shall we?"

An hour later, Epaphras is escorting me to dinner with my gargoyles following behind. He takes me to a smaller room than I have been to thus far for dinner. The room is cozy, intimate. He pulls out one of the two chairs set at the small, round table for me and once I am seated, he tells me the king will be here momentarily. I watch him leave and then take a good look at the room, as if focusing on that will help me relax while I wait. What if he doesn't show up? I get a sudden insane urge to laugh, because how many people could say they were stood up by the king? Focus Valdís!

Table. Very shiny. Flowers in a vase, but the stems are short as is the vase. The chairs are ornate on the backs but very cushioned if the one I am sitting in is anything to go by. The walls look to be a dark red, but that may be partly because of the candles. Luckily, the ceiling is high, so it isn't heating the room. The door opens and his scent hits me. I close my eyes and inhale. Every fiber of my being lights up with lust every time I smell him. I want to ravish him, claim him, make him mine; and I have the strangest urge to bite him. I can't even imagine where the hell that comes from. When I open my eyes, I find him watching me. His eyes intense and his nostrils flared, he says, "Why do you do that when I get near you?"

"Do what?"

"Why do you close your eyes and inhale like you smell something delicious suddenly?"

And there's the blushing again. Super. I focus intently on the flowers before me, saying, "Well, it's you. Every time you come around, I get hit with this scent and it smells amazing. I really, oh isn't that enough explanation? You just smell good. Okay?"

I never heard him move, but suddenly he is whispering in my ear, "You don't have to tell me what it does to you. I can smell the way it makes you wet. Now you can think about how much that smell makes me want to lick you till you scream my name."

My head tilts of its own accord and I bare my neck to him, even as I feel an almost unbearable need to bite him. What is wrong with me?

He licks my neck, and I shiver. Then he is on the other

side of the table, sitting down as someone walks in with a large tray. It's all I can do to get myself together while this guy gets our soup set before us. By the time he leaves, I am a little more in control. I watch as he begins to eat his soup, those lips... Don't think about that. I dip my spoon into my own soup. As I do, I remember something my father told me when I was younger. "May I ask you a personal question?"

He lifts a brow and then nods.

"My father told me stories about you and your brothers when I was younger. He always mentioned that part of the gift the Goddess gave you was more a curse than gift because you must drink blood to stay alive. But, if that's true, how are you able to eat food? I apologize if that is a silly question, but I figure my chance of ever getting to ask something like this is none after tonight, so I may as well shoot my shot."

His lips curve into a smile as he says, "Worried I'll drink your blood?" The way I tipped my head and bared my neck flashes in my mind and I have to laugh. "It is true that my brothers and I must drink blood to survive to some extent. The blood allows us to renew ourselves in a way. Food, that nourishes us in ways the blood does not. Without drinking blood, we would eventually wither and die. But our Goddess ensured that would not happen, because if we go without for too long, we get crazed for it and risk killing our donor. So we try to avoid that. I can see the curiosity burning in you, go ahead and ask."

I grin at him, saying, "Am I so obvious? You called them donors. Are they willing?"

He nods, "Yes, in general. Though we have no problems taking someone unwilling if they are annoying us."

"Fair enough. How often do you need to drink? Can you drink from animals or just humans? Do you have a preference? Do different people taste different?"

He waits to answer while the guy that brought the soup brings us the main course and clears away the soup. The guy leaves and I sink my fork into a bit of fish as he says, "I need to drink a few times a month. Animal or human is possible. I prefer humans because the animals piss me off way less. Every one tastes different."

I think about that as I chew and swallow. "If I understand correctly, you mostly don't kill the donors, correct?" He nods and I press on, "Do you have preferred donors?"

His eyes burn as he stares at me and I can't look away as he says, "Not in a very long time, but yes, some can be favorites."

Swallowing, my throat suddenly dry, I reach for the glass before me and drink deeply. The wine is sweet and cool; it goes down easily. I think maybe I should ask about anything else. This is getting too intense for me to be able to focus. "I, ahem, I imagine running the kingdom is even more paperwork than our little portion is. You all cycle out. How do you keep it all organized?"

He smiles at me, asking, "Do I scare you?" My breath catches in my throat as I shake my head yes and he laughs, "I don't think I do. You don't," he inhales deeply, "smell like fear right now. You smell like lust and fire and the sweetest cream begging to be lapped up. Come, let us walk. You cloud my thoughts with the scent of you in here, and all I can think about is what is under that skirt."

He stands and extends a hand to me. I stand on legs much more wobbly than I would have expected and take his hand. He guides me to his side before leading me out the door. His hand is cool, and his skin like silk under my fingers, though I can feel the steel underneath it all. I want to explore the rest of him, but he hasn't asked me to, no matter how much we have been circling around it. Plus, Epaphras warned me about this and I would like to not die.

The gardens have really cranked up the blooming lately and are incredibly fragrant with the scents of a few hundred flowers blooming. We walk through the gardens and he points out different flowers to me. Telling me where they used to grow wild and why they don't now. I can't imagine how he is able to focus on pulling all these minor facts about flowers out of his brain when I can barely string two words together. The scent of him mixed with the flowers is almost intoxicating. Then my eyes drift down his body and I notice the bulge at the front of his pants. My breath catches as heat pools in my core and I tear my eyes away.

His words falter, and I can hear him inhale. I find myself dangling in the air, his hands around my waist as he holds me up in front of him, "How am I supposed to concentrate on telling you about the damned flowers if you are so turned on it's all I can smell? What is setting you off like this?"

My face explodes into flames, and I struggle with words, but finally manage, "It's your scent. Mixed with the flowers, it is like an aphrodisiac. I can't help it, and it has been entirely too long since I had sex with anyone. It is no picnic from this side. I am sorry it is messing up our evening. I don't mean to make you uncomfortable."

The surprise on his face would be comical any other time. He sets me down on my feet, hands lingering to ensure that I have my balance. "Valdís, I can take care of that for you right now, and we can continue our stroll through the gardens."

I am a little confused. Does he mean to fuck me here in the gardens and then continue the walk? I don't care if he does. Relief would be glorious. "Yes, please," I tell him, though I am unsure of what I am getting myself into. He grins and takes my hand, leading me to a bench set in the bushes where he sits down and guides me to stand in front of him. He doesn't look especially comfortable on the low bench, but I am still confused. His hands go to my thighs and he starts to slowly bunch the fabric of my skirt in his hands. My breathing hitches and gets faster as he gets the bottom edge in his hand. His fingers on my thighs and my skirt still bunched in his hands, he pushes it up, tucking it in my waist before he looks at the prize he has revealed. A hiss of breath rushes out of his mouth when he sees my naked pussy before him. Not a pair of panties in sight.

"Darlin', you know what I like," he murmurs as he stares. One hand goes to my ass, gripping it comfortably while the other lifts my leg and puts it on his shoulder, bringing me so close I can feel his breath on my pussy. His other hand goes to my ass, and he tells me, "Don't worry about falling. I got you." His lips and tongue delve into my pussy and he immediately hits my clit. It is like electricity running through my body. I cry out as the first orgasm in a long time hits me and his mouth works my pussy so expertly that I seem to stay at that peak. My hips involuntarily grinding and pulling away from his face even as my fingers thread into his hair, hanging on for dear life as he wrings every ounce of pleasure from my body.

My legs turn to jello and I can't even hold myself up anymore and I drenched him in my come. He finally releases me, pulling his lips and tongue away from my body. I whimper as he does and I don't know if it is from pleasure or sadness that he has stopped pleasuring me.

He moves slowly to lower the leg that was on his shoulder, holding me upright the whole time. Both of my feet are on the ground now, but I am still wobbly. He pulls my skirt out of my waistband and moves his hands out of the way one at a time, he wipes his face with one hand and motions for me to sit with the other. On his lap. I try to move to sit next to him and he scowls at me, saying, "I just had your pussy in my mouth. I think you can sit on my lap."

"But what if I get your clothing messy?"

"They wash. Or they went to a good cause. Either way, don't you worry about that and sit that fine ass on my lap. That is an order. From your king."

I guess I can't argue with that, so I sit down. His hand immediately cups my ass and pulls me closer. It is strange and exhilarating to have sex of any sort with someone that can handle my weight. He fully supported my weight as I was drenching his face in my cum. Most men would have crumpled and I would be sporting a head injury right now. I lean on his chest, resting my head on his shoulder. His other arm moves to pull me closer, and stays there on my side. I have the strangest urge to bite him again, and I don't understand it at all. I have never had the urge to bite any of my lovers, not once.

My breathing is slowing and honestly, I could sleep here. I am so relaxed. I guess he could tell because he rubs my arm a bit, saying, "Come, let's finish this walk."

Standing up, I find that my legs are not in fact made of jelly and they do work again. He adjusts himself discreetly as he stands. I definitely hope I can help to ease his discomfort. I wonder... Fuck it, I'm going to ask. "You know, if you wanted to go back to my room and take care of that now instead of wandering the grounds, we can do that."

His brows raise as he says, "Oh, really?"

"It looks incredibly uncomfortable to have your cock so hard and so confined. I have a nice soft space that would readily welcome it."

Next thing I know, he has swept me up in his arms and is carrying me back toward the castle. I know my gargoyles are following behind us, watching this, but I don't care for once. He takes me to his room, his guards opening his door and closing it securely behind us. Inside, he tosses me on his bed, I land with arms and legs splayed. He is above me on his hands and knees before I can move.

My eyes follow the line of his body, past the tempting curve of his neck to see his eyes, intense and nearly glowing in the dim light of the room. I can see the tips of his teeth peeking out between those luscious lips, and I push up to kiss him. The instant our lips touch, fire explodes through my body as he presses me down to the bed, his mouth seeking every inch of mine, his teeth pricking at my lips and tongue. I taste my blood in our mouths and it stokes the fire even hotter.

He growls, his hands finding mine, tugging them up over my head and holding them in place with one hand. The other traces its way back down my arm to cup a breast. He breaks the kiss. I am sucking air like I was deprived of it when he snatches the shirt open. His mouth is on my nipple, sucking hard, and my back arches, pressing into his mouth. His hand finds the waist of my skirt and tugs it down. I lift my ass to help it slide off. He gets it down to my knees and I pull my legs up one at a time to get rid of the damned thing. His hand comes back to my knee and slides up my thigh as he lets go of my nipple with a small popping sound before he moves to the other one. Sucking hard and letting his teeth prick my breast lightly on either side as his two fingers slide into my pussy.

The base of his palm is grinding on my clit as his fingers curl inside me and I can't stop from coming on his fingers. My hips bucking and writhing as his hand stays in place, wringing more and more pleasure from my body. He releases my breast and eases the base of his palm away from my body. I relax, my knees dropping open. Then he releases my hands and moves to position himself with his mouth just a breath away from my pussy. I look down at him, "You can't, it's so sensitive already."

He growls, "I can, I will, and you will love it." His mouth descends onto my pussy as I watch. He licks from entrance to clit with his tongue broad and flat. It feels so good my hips rock into his mouth. He hums as his mouth claims me once again. The pleasure is so intense that all I can do is moan and shiver as his arms hold my hips where he wants them.

An eternity or a moment later he lifts his mouth from my throbbing pussy, I sigh in contentment. My eyes slide closed as I listen to him moving around. Then he grabs my legs and lifts them, his knees going to either side of my ass before he sets my legs down with my feet on the bed. He strokes his cock along my slit and my hips rock up toward him. He slides it back down my slit and this time pushes into me slowly. The slow stretch almost makes me cum again, and he presses hard on my clit with his thumb.

The orgasm rockets through my body as my hips rock on his cock, making him groan. His hands move to grip my hips and he slams into me. The walls of my pussy keep contracting in orgasm around his cock and it feels so good I think I might die right here as he pounds away at me. His mouth finds mine, tongue delving deeply as he fucks me hard and fast. His mouth rips away from mine and he roars as he slams into me one more time, staying buried within me as he cums.

Knox

I wake up to her luscious, delicious body curled up next to me, wrapped up in my arms, and fear hits me like a brick. She feels so right next to me. Easing my arm out from under her, I grab my pants and stuff my legs in them as I cross the room. I close the door in silence, then I am off. Striding down the hall without a destination in mind. I just need to be away from her. I knew I shouldn't get close to her.

I couldn't resist her. After I nearly killed her in the hall running into her, after we nearly had sex right there in front of everyone, I had to have her. Had to see her, talk to her, smell her, taste her. What have I done? She can't be the one. It just isn't possible.

Yet, even now. Even now, I want to run back to my room and take her. Again. Bite her and make her my own. If she is the one, if she is, everything will change. We all just got to a point where we could stave off some of the boredom by going to visit the rest of the world. What if I dive into this and she isn't the one? How will I be able to go back to the life I had before? I can't. I can't go back to that and I can't stay away from her.

What am I going to do? How do I know if she is the one? I know our people live longer than the average human, but a few hundred years is nothing compared to how long I have already lived. Whatever happens, we have to make sure she is safe. Her mother and Ingemar must be stopped. Permanently. With at least one decision made, I head for my office. I'll have Epaphras bring me some clothing.

* * *

Valdís

He is gone when I wake up. The room is dark and quiet, why did he leave? The sun is barely up. He can't have needed to tend to business that early, can he? I don't have a shirt to wear anymore, because he ripped mine open. Epaphras walks in and turns on a light just as I was about to get out of bed and I snatch the sheet back in front of me. He looks surprised to see me and then some other things flit across his face that I don't understand, but he asks, "Why are you in here? You aren't supposed to be in this wing."

He says it without anger or really any inflection in his voice, but suddenly I know why he left the room so early and my stomach drops. I really thought he was different. As I feel the burn of tears to come in my eyes and I refuse to cry about this motherfucker so instead I tell Epaphras, "I was invited last night. I didn't mean to fall asleep, so sorry. And I will return to my room now." I scoop up my clothing and walk right out the door, as naked as the day I was born.

I hear one of his room guards behind me exclaim in a loud whisper, "Holy shit, look at that ass!" I feel a little gratified. I parade my ass right through the castle to my own room, where my guards wait. They are masterful at keeping their facial expressions neutral as one of them opens the door for me. I tell them as I walk through, "I would like to have all my meals in my room today, I am not feeling well." One of them says he will see to it while the other closes the door behind me. The tears that have been threatening this entire time begin to spill over as I drop my clothing on the floor and head for a good shower cry. I will scrub every trace of that man off of me and he can go fuck himself for all he will ever see that I care again.

Thirteen

V aldís

* * *

The shower was long, and I scrubbed every inch of my body even as my tears mixed with the shower water. I was just so drained after that I crawled into the bed and slept. Now that I am awake again and my heart hurts, I can't decide if I want to cry, rage, or run away. Sitting up in the bed, I see that I apparently slept through breakfast as there is what appears to be a tray of lunch set on the table. I guess Epaphras is done talking to me as well. And that is just more than I can handle. I slide out of the bed and head for the closet. My clothing was set on shelves toward the back and those are the only ones I am taking with me.

Whatever decision he is going to make about my petition, he can make it without my presence here. Maybe it will go more favorably for me if I am gone anyway, since he is so obviously done with me and doesn't want me around. Dressing and packing takes very little time. I step out of my door and my gargoyles are still there, they see me and the one on the left says, "Um, are you leaving?"

"Yes, actually, I am. Suddenly, the castle feels like I don't belong here. He can figure out my petition without me being here, and I am sure you guys have better things to do than stand guard over me all day."

"If you'll forgive my saying so, ma'am, I don't think you should leave. Whoever is after you means to hurt you and whether or not you and the king are getting along, he will keep you safe."

Tears sting my eyes again, "Yeah? Who is going to protect me from him? I can't stay here and let him walk all over my heart. It isn't like I don't have money and I can make it on my own. I just wanted to do right by my people. But I guess I'll probably fail at that, too."

I walk away and they follow behind. I guess they kind of have orders to do so and I am not trying to get them in trouble.

Valdís

I manage to give my guards the slip by making them wait outside the kitchen while I say goodbye to cook, I really did say goodbye to cook and he told me about some cousins up north that would welcome me if I needed a minute. I left through the door at the other end of the kitchen and headed for the front door. I wanted them to be safe from his wrath, and if I was at least to blame then they shouldn't get in much trouble, if any.

I am nearly to the front door when the scent hits me. I push through it, hoping to get out the door where he won't see me. Pulling one of the large doors open I am stepping through when his hand wraps around my throat, pushing me back against the door frame, "Where do you think you are going? I distinctly remember leaving you in my bed this morning and before that telling you to stay with the castle walls, with your guards. Now tell me little trouble, where did you think you were going?"

He has me pinned to the door frame by my neck, not squeezing, yet. But the threat is there and my body, traitor that it is, is all for it. His questions just piss me off and I decide to answer them the way I would for any guy this maddening. "Yes, you left me alone in your bed. Left me to wake up alone to people asking me what I was doing in a section of the castle forbidden to me! While they were fetching your twice damned shirt! After walking back to my rooms NAKED because some jackass shredded my top and my dignity, I decided that you can help me or not, but you don't fucking well need me here to do so."

His hand softens and his mouth falls open as I hurl my accusations. He didn't know. Then he snatches me to his body and inside the castle as some things thunk into the door frame I was just standing in front of, he shouts, "Attack! We are under attack!" Men go running past as he whisks me off and shoves me in a closet. "You stay here until

I return or I swear to the Goddess herself, I will spank your ass till you beg for mercy."

He slams the door before I can tell him I'll just like it if he does that. When he returns within a few minutes and opens the door, looking surprised when I am still standing there in the closet. He reaches in and grabs my hand, pulling me along to stand behind the closed door. There are a ridiculous amount of guards all over the place right now as he points to the space I had been standing in just moments ago. There are three crossbow bolts buried in the wood and he says, "This is why I want you safe inside the castle until this is done. I can't save you if you get shot by three damn crossbows."

"I'm not here so you can save me! I am here so you can save my people! I am not the important piece here!"

He roars at me, "You are to me!"

My heart breaks all over again as I say, "If I was that important, you wouldn't have had your people kicking me out of your room for you this morning, Knox. I wouldn't have been there alone when they came for your clothing because you were too scared to come get it yourself. You don't have to worry, I understand now. I won't read anything into your advances beyond lust." I slip out of his hold as he stares at me and I hold my head as high as I can while I walk to my rooms. My gargoyles fall in with me as I go and I tell them, "I apologize for ditching you. I thought it better if you were able to claim you didn't know."

The walk to my room is forever, since all I want is for him to come to me. Maybe even apologize like he understands what he did wrong. But no. I make it all the way to my room with my gargoyles for company. They take up their posts on either side of my door as I close it behind me. Leaning against it for just a moment as I let the tears slip down my face. Crossing the room is a monumental effort, but I crawl into the bed and under the blankets to the one escape left to me.

Fourteen

V aldís

* * *

I wake up to him entering my room, and I croak out, "What the fuck are you doing in here? Get out."

"I couldn't stay away from you. Don't you see what you do to me?"

I lean up, elbows on the bed behind me, "Well, let's see... As far as I can tell, I make you all happy in places that are very inconvenient for the rest of you. That is fine. But I need you to leave me alone if you don't mean any of this. Just go make your damn decision on the petition and let me go."

He growls and in a blink is next to the bed and has me upright, our bodies pressed against one another. Every nerve ending in my body is tuned to all the places our bodies are touching, all the little bits of friction. He looks so angry and I can't help myself, saying, "Now what? Going to spank me if I don't act the way you want me to? Or maybe you'd just like to fuck me senseless?"

"Stop talking Valdís."

"Or what?" His hand comes to the back of my head and fingers twine in my hair, he pulls my head back and lightly nips at my neck. I moan, and he releases my hair, both hands going to the hem of my shirt. He starts pushing it up, and my arms lift to allow him to pull it off of me. His hands make quick work of the straps fastening my bra and it joins my shirt as floor decoration. His hands are a blur as he unbuttons my pants. He lifts me off the bed and sets me before him and his hands go right back to the waist of my pants, pushing them down over my hips and kneeling before me to pull my foot out of each leg. Instead of standing, he grabs my ass with both hands and buries his tongue in my pussy. I gasp and my fingers bury themselves in his hair.

His tongue swirls and delves deeper until he can go no farther, so he withdraws and as he stands, he tosses me onto the bed. I yelp in surprise and then his mouth is on my pussy again and all thoughts leave my mind as he floods my body with sensations. The suction of his mouth, his tongue as it works my clit to a fever pitch, the hand holding my hips; the fingers finding my entrance and curling up to hit another sensitive spot. It isn't long before I am writhing and twitching under his ministrations, my breath coming in gasps as he takes me to new heights of pleasure. When he finally takes his mouth from my pussy, I lay there, spent. Until he flips me over and snatches my ass into the air by my hips. He strokes his cock along my dripping pussy, making me moan and push back toward his cock.

He moves the head to my entrance, saying, "Tell me you want it," he growls at me.

I moan as my hips rock to try and get a little more of him inside me, moaning, "I want your cock."

The words barely leave my lips when he plunges into me, sinking his cock into my velvety folds. He pistons in and out of me as he grabs my hair while holding my hip and uses it to pull me up so my back is against him. The hand on my hip moves to my clit and starts doing things that have me crying out in ecstasy. He pulls my head to one side, baring my neck and I don't even care if he were to drain me dry as long as he fucked me like this the whole time. I feel his teeth scrape across my skin and a massive orgasm hits me, my whole body convulsing before my pussy goes wild, clenching around his cock and he slams into me with a roar, I feel his cock pulsing inside me. We collapse on the bed, sated and exhausted for the moment.

Within minutes, I feel him withdraw from my pussy, causing it to quiver as he does. Then he moves to the side of the bed, puts his head in his hands and starts to mope. I sit up to verify what I think is happening and yes; he is really moping on the side of the bed not five minutes after we had some really magnificent sex. What the hell is wrong with him? You know what? I don't even care. Let him sit here and figure that shit out. I am going to go see cook about some food.

I move to the other side of the bed and get down.

Crossing the room to the closet, I grab some clothes and start the process of stuffing myself into them.

I am just putting on the pants when he says, "What the fuck do you think you are doing?"

"What the fuck does it look like I am doing?"

"It looks like you are getting dressed and the only reason I can think of for that is you want those clothes ripped off of you this time."

I cannot believe this guy! "You are not fucking well touching me again, you moody bastard! You left me last time and this time you are over at the edge of the bed moping like fucking me was some goddess damned chore! There are plenty of people out there that want to fuck me and are grateful—"

He crosses the room in a heartbeat, "Let's get one thing straight now, princess. No one else will be fucking that pretty pussy of yours. You are mine."

"The fuck I am! You don't get to claim me and then act like it's a mistake every time we fuck! I came here to help my people, not get plowed by someone that doesn't want me."

"Doesn't want you — is that what you think is going on here? Princess, want is too weak a word for what I feel about you. I am still trying to process that, because the possibility of you being more could change everything. Everything! If you are more, if you are a mate, our world is going to explode. I like my life, it is finally pretty great. But you show up with your petition and I can't seem to stay away from you. Even now, your blood calls to me and," his nostrils flare as he sniffs the air, "that pussy is begging for the release I can give it."

"Too fucking bad for you, my pussy isn't in charge! I don't give a single fuck about any of that. You can process your shit without shitting on me!"

Knox

My shoulders drop and I tell her, "You're right. I can and I will. I am almost one hundred percent certain that you are my mate," as well as my brother's mate, but I don't think you are ready for that conversation, "and you deserve better than how I have treated you."

"Mate? Are you drunk?"

Chuckling, I tell her, "No. Not drunk. I have known for a long time that there would be one woman for me, one woman that would be my mate. A woman whose scent would drive me wild with desire and who would have no fear of me though she should," I say, eyeing her. She lifts her chin and crosses her arms over those gorgeous breasts of hers and I struggle to bring my eyes back to hers, "and many other things that tell me you are likely the one. I apologize for being an ass."

"Any chance you can promise not to be again?"

I shake my head, saying, "No, it is pretty guaranteed that I will do it again."

I wait as she appears to think this over. Finally she nods, "Okay. We can talk about this. I can't deny that something about you draws me and the smell of you can stop me in my tracks. However, you're king. I am not going through the embarrassment of being kicked out of your rooms because they are trying to follow your bullshit rules again. And I am not going to bow to your will," I raise an eyebrow and grin at her, "outside the bedroom or while in court. And if you use your power against me, it is off. You and your delicious scents can go fuck yourself at that point."

"Fair enough. I will remove all the restrictions on your movement, but I would ask that you not go into my brother's rooms without their invitation."

"Why would your brothers invite me to their rooms? That's weird. Why would I go in there without invitation? Look, I am not going to your room even without you inviting me. I just don't want to be treated like a creeper if you leave me in there alone."

"Let me take you out. I have a nice boat, I can take you out on the ocean. I can even get you to the ocean with no one seeing us go." As I grin at her, I say, "We could check on how far we could get the boat to rock?"

She laughs and I know she has forgiven me. I leave her to dress while I go fetch my own clothing and send people to get the boat ready. Making it quick, I find Epaphras along the way, "She is now allowed free roam of the castle, still with a guard for her safety. I am allowing her in my room as well. I have not banned her from my brother's rooms, though I asked her not to enter them without invitation."

Epaphras cuts his eyes at me, asking, "And do we think she will get invitations?"

"I do. I have not told her about the queen's room either. And I won't any time soon. If she displays any curiosity about it, you may tell her the barest outline of what it is for. If she asks if it is forbidden to her, it is not.

But I would prefer that she discover and explore it on her own and in her own time."

"Understood. So you think the Queen is finally arrived."

Sighing, I tell him, "It feels like it. But I don't trust that I am not just grasping at someone that finally piques my interest, smells nice, and isn't continually throwing herself at me. It has been so long, I don't know if I can tell the difference. I think my brother's reactions will let me know if she is just someone I could care about for a time or if she is the queen."

* * *

Collecting Valdís from her room, we walk arm in arm through the castle and outside, crossing to the garage. Our garage is small above ground, but below is another story. She is confused when I lead her past the car to a wall and press a specific tile off to the side. She smiles widely and is very excited when the panel opens to reveal the elevator. We get in and are in the lower section of the garage quickly. Guiding her to the passenger seat of the first car I get to, I move to the driver's seat and hit the remote once I am seated. Low lights come to life, lighting the way to our closest place by the ocean. She is silent and watches the tunnel fly by as I drive.

The drive that would be an hour and a half above ground takes us a mere half hour. The garage on the other end is much like the one we left behind at the castle. Our dock is within a few minutes' walk through our property. As we walk, she looks around at the different plants growing on the property. She points to a particular species of fern, saying, "I thought you said this one didn't grow wild anymore?"

"It doesn't. This is more of our land, we cultivate those plants everywhere."

"Oh, and I guess that is your boat there as well?"

"It is." She looks apprehensive and I ask, "Ready to go out?"

"How many times have you been out in that boat?"

"Many. How many times have you been out on a boat?"

"Zero. Zero times."

"Well, we'll go slowly. Get you on board and see how you feel after a bit. Before we leave the dock. If you do ok, we'll go a little ways out and see how that goes. Don't worry, we will take it slow and if this isn't for you, then we will stay on dry land."

"Really? You would do that for me?"

"Yes? What the hell kind of people — never mind. I know what kind of people you have been around. If you are uncomfortable, we will change the outing. Period." I can't believe these people she is related to, what assholes. We stroll down the dock to the boat. I love this boat, it's a good size sailboat, though we have a motor in it as well. I christened her The Dazzler, and she has dazzled me with her maneuverability and seaworthiness.

Valdís walks up the gangplank and onto my boat, her hand on my arm a little more firmly. Once on the boat though, she released my arm and walked over to the opposite side of the boat and stands there for a time with her hands on the railing. Leaving her to decide if she can handle being on a boat, I start pre-sail checks. My guys will have already done this, but I like to do it anyway. I might notice something they didn't. My checks go a lot faster because of vampire speed and when I finish, I go to her. "Are you all right? What is the verdict?"

She turns to me with a smile that could light up the darkest night, "I love this! The ocean is so beautiful. Let's go out in it and see if my body can handle it. I think it can. This is great!"

She is nearly vibrating with joy, and I love it. I take her hand and guide her to a seat, saying, "I'll get the engine going and take us out a little way. If you start to feel ill, just yell. Anything. I will turn the boat around as gently as possible."

"Where will you be?"

I point, "Right up there. If you are ok with this, then you can wander mostly where you please."

"Mostly?"

"I assume you don't want to get hit by the sails," I tell her with a shrug. She laughs as I leave her to get us going.

* * *

Valdís

We were both so concerned about how I would do on

the water and I love it. This is the best thing ever and I could stay out here forever. After a quick check to make sure I am ok out in the water as opposed to moored at the dock, we set sail. Mostly, I sit toward the front of the boat and just enjoy as he guides us through the water. I turn to watch him as he moves around the boat doing things. Honestly, he could be getting the boat ready to sink and I wouldn't know until it started to sink.

He doesn't seem to want me dead currently, so I am probably safe. He lets the boat coast to a stop, well, as stopped as anything gets when surrounded by ocean. He brings a basket of food out and sets it on the deck, "I thought we could have a little picnic on the deck?"

I love this, the man wants to feed me! "Yes, lets!"

He grins at me and darts off, coming back with a wooden box. He unfolds it and we have a low table with suction cups on the bottom of the legs. He sets the table up and I move from my seat to be near the table and help with unpacking the basket. He brought what looks like mead, the bottle isn't labeled with a name, only a date. An assortment of fruits chopped into bite size pieces, cheeses, some raw fish on ice, and a loaf of bread.

As we eat he tells me stories of the parties they used to have, back when all twelve of them were still alive. "What happened to them? I know there are rumors, but no one knows what happened, or if they do they aren't talking. Why did they disappear?"

His face contorts with rage, "What do you mean no one knows?" he near shouts at me. "So many of them were there! It was the reason we closed the damned borders and why the

Goddess made the world think our continent sank to the bottom of the ocean!" He gets up and paces, "No one knows? Really? Have we been so oblivious in our grief that we missed the coverup of the murder of our brothers? Some of our own people were part of the plot. We think there may have been even more that we just couldn't find evidence linking them to the crimes." His face is heart broken as he turns to look at me, "We sacrificed everything to save our people and they murdered most of us. Now they pretend it never happened?"

I stood while he spoke, with the thought that I might need to follow his pacing to hear it all. When he stopped and turned to me, all I could do is go to him and wrap my arms around him, saying, "I am so sorry. We can tell people. We can spread the stories." His arms wrap around me, lifting me and holding me tightly against him, "My father told me the old stories, but every time he started to tell me why we only have five kings out of the twelve we started with, mother would always come in and say that he was telling tales out of hand, he shouldn't fill my head with nonsense."

He says, his voice muffled by my shoulder, "Your mother should take the long jump from the cliffs on the north end of the continent. The rocks would welcome her."

I laugh, saying, "Well, that would solve some problems. But it would leave Ingemar still trying to marry me off to his troll of a son, Pelos."

Knox squeezes me a little tighter, saying, "You will not be marrying anyone's son, troll or not. You belong to me."

"Is that so? And I get no say in the matter?" I ask him

with a laugh because I really have no problem with this, if he means it.

"Too late for that. Should have said no before I ever tasted you. Now you're mine."

Valdís

The return to shore is a little more heavy than the leaving. I stand with him as he guides the boat in. Guards and Epaphras are waiting on the dock, they look anxious. As we draw near Knox tosses ropes to the guards and they tie it up as Knox darts back to handle the controls. As soon as the boat stops guards jump across and extend the walkway. We hurry to the dock where Epaphras waits. "Sire, there have been explosions at the castle."

Knox tenses, "Where?"

Epaphras swallows, "The first one was the wall of her bedroom. People were seen leaving the scene via the new hole in the wall. The second was in the cells. The two guards you captured in the prior attempt to remove Valdís from the castle were killed in the explosion, as was one of our own." He glances over at me before returning his attention to Knox, saying, "And um, Eirene has sent a demand for her daughter to be returned to her. She apparently has concerns for Valdís's arranged marriage falling thru for chastity concerns as she is here with you, unmarried and her being so feeble minded."

I watch Knox as Epaphras delivers this news. His face grows hard and his fists clench. "Epaphras, go back to the castle. Have Valdís's things moved to the unused room in the king's wing."

"Sire, are you sure? That room?"

"I am. Now go and make for damn certain the castle is secured. I don't want an unauthorized fly roaming the halls."

Epaphras strides off, one of the guards with him, while the other three stay with us.

Fifteen

V aldís

* * *

We walk rather quickly up the dock and down the path to the garage. I wait until we start down in the elevator before I ask, "What room am I going to in the king's wing?"

He sighs, "There is one room," he opens the door for me and I get in, watching as he rounds the car and gets in. The guards have left already in their own car. Knox continues as he sends us flying through the tunnel, saying, "One room that has never been used. It was always waiting for its owner. I am pretty sure it is going to welcome you."

"Wait, why do you have a room waiting for someone? And what do you mean you think it will welcome me? Rooms don't welcome people."

"This one is waiting and it will welcome its owner. I think you are that owner."

We arrive at the garage at the other end and I decide to see what happens in this room. Maybe Knox is off his rocker after living so long? He is hurrying me through everything and we are quickly walking across the courtyard when something hits me in the back and wraps around me, clutching my torso. I yell, "Knox!" as I fly through the air. Suddenly, I crash into something and darkness welcomes me.

Knox

Valdís shouts my name as she is snatched through the air, away from me. I can only watch in horror as she hits a tree and falls. I run across the courtyard, leaping to the top of the wall in time to see a car roar away. Two guards make the leap to stand atop the wall with me. "Bring a car and my bike," I tell the one to the right. "Catch up with us." I leap from the wall and race for the place where the car turned, hoping to keep sight of the damn thing. I have to get her back!

I hear the other guard behind me, feet pounding the pavement as he follows. As I round the corner just in time to see the car take another corner. I put on more speed, but when I reach the corner, there is nothing. No car. My bike roars up, a car and two more bikes following. I tell them, "I am going to try to follow the scent, but split up and see if you can find anything." I hop on my bike and try to follow the scent even as it fades.

·   ·   ·

Ingemar

The stairs are tedious. I should have an elevator installed. The climb to the third floor is worth it this time, though. This time I get to view my little prize. I open the door to find she is still unconscious. Her hands are tied behind her and her feet are tied separately to her hands.

She is lovely, all soft curves. Running a hand along a thigh exposed by the shorts she wears, I think about getting a head start on impregnating her.

Unfortunately, my son walks in at that moment. I snatch my hand away from her and turn to him, saying, "Come to see your soon to be bride?"

"Yes. And you?"

"Just checking on my future daughter-in-law. Get the servants to untie her and bring her some food when she wakes, and you continue to monitor her. Oh, and send a note to dear Eirene, announcing the wedding tomorrow. We wouldn't want her to miss her daughter's wedding." I follow him out, as I know he would not trust me with her right now. While he continues down to the first floor, I stay on the second. There is a delightful maid that should be making beds right now and she is curvy enough to pass for my daughter-in-law if I take her from behind.

Eirene

"I can't believe that bastard double-crossed me!" I throw another of my husband's prized books across the room. Eume jumps, frightened. I sneer at her. "That bastard has her and could ruin our chances at reclaiming the inheritance that should have been mine!" I wave the notice that bastard sent me, "And the nerve of him to send a wedding notice! I know he has always wanted this place, greedy fuck that he is!" There is a knock at the door, "Come in!"

Flavi escorts the judge I sent for into the room and I tell him, "Welcome! So glad to see you, Leesan!" I kiss his cheek, "I need your help, desperately. Will you help me?"

He stutters, single all his life because he gets exceedingly nervous around women, "I will help any way I can."

"Excellent, come sit." I lead him to the chair before my desk, waving out of his sight for Eume to leave the room. She glides out silently, closing the door without a sound. I get him settled and I lean against the desk before him. "Now, do you recall my eldest daughter, Valdís?"

He pauses to think and says, "I think I do, strange girl. She was always trying to run outside. Very unladylike."

"Yes, exactly. She was always a strange girl and as she got older, well, the strangeness developed into illness. Now, Ingemar has taken her and I am afraid he means to marry her to his son in order to steal her inheritance from the family. My husband adored her and went outside the usual way of things with the inheritance. Now it is in jeopardy as Ingemar plans to marry her to his son. Could you, would you, please help me save my home?"

He flushes as I lean toward him, saying, "I will do whatever I can. What do you need from me?"

"All I need is for you to sign this order I had prepared, saying that Valdís is not competent to hold the inheritance and it should go to me. So that I can maintain our holdings and see that she is well taken care of. As I believe Ingemar will not marry her to his son once he knows he cannot claim the holdings that way. It is really all for her protection."

The man is really too easy. My cleavage is barely out, and he is breathing hard already as he says, "Yes. I can easily do that and have the filing back dated a few days. Will, um, will that do for you?"

"That will do just perfectly. Let's get that done now, shall we?" I smile widely at him as I tug him up from the chair. Guiding him to come around the desk and stand over me as I sign my portion of the papers and the copies I had made. I allow him to stand there and ogle down my shirt as I do. It all just works so much easier if he thinks less. Once I have finished, I move a little to the side so that he can sign and stamp things. He is such a good boy, he doesn't even sweat on me as he works. He is incredibly flustered by the time he finishes. I pick up his copy and fold it in thirds, slipping it into an envelope and licking it as I look in his eyes. It looks like he may have had a minor accident as his eyes rolled up and he twitched a bit. I pretend not to notice, as his breathing is heavier than it should be right now.

I turn and write his name across the front of the envelope, allowing him ample time to stare at my ass. So much easier to do things like this now that my husband is dead. Turning back to him, I slide the envelope into the hand that was drifting toward my ass, saying, "Here you go. Could you please get that filed now? I need to send a copy to Ingemar and he will be checking in the morning."

"Oh, yes! Let me go tend to that now." He starts to

leave and turns back, "Do, um, I mean, would it be possible, may I call on you again?"

I don't really like the little shit but, it couldn't hurt to have a judge in my pocket. "Of course you may. Just do schedule it with my people first. I have been dreadfully busy since my husband died so suddenly."

He bobs his head, saying, "Yes, of course. I will get this," he holds up the envelope, "taken care of right now."

"Wonderful, thank you dear sir."

As he closes the door behind himself I sit down at my desk and fold another copy into thirds, stuffing it into an envelope, this one I scrawl Ingemar across the front. Standing, I take the envelope to the door and call out, "Flavi!"

The girl comes running, "Yes ma'am?"

"Have this taken to Ingemar now. I don't need a response, as I am retiring to my rooms. I do not wish to be disturbed for the rest of the evening unless it is urgent, understand?"

"I do," she says as she bobs a quick curtsy and takes off for the head guard's office.

Sixteen

*** * ***

Valdís

My head feels like it is split in pieces and all the pieces are being hit with a hammer repeatedly. The room is bright as I try to open my eyes, and what little I see I don't recognize. My eyelids feel a lot like sandpaper, but I keep blinking, seeing the room in blurry snapshots. As my vision clears, I see a small room, all white. Moving hurts like hell as I struggle to sit up. The door opens and Pelos walks in.

Of course, it's Pelos. Great. These assholes. He smiles at me when he sees I am sitting up and conscious, "Valdís, excellent. How are you feeling?"

"I feel like hell. Being slammed against something during a kidnapping isn't very good for the body."

"Kidnapping? What kidnapping? We just brought you home, where you belong. You can't stay in that castle forever as the king's hostage. We simply sped up the process. Besides, we can't have everyone thinking that my bride is the king's whore."

I can't believe he is so delusional. "Pelos, I am not marrying you. I would rather burn this place to the ground than be your bride."

"Ah, and you do not deny you are the king's whore? Interesting. Hopefully, you learned something good from him that will please me tomorrow night after we are wed."

"You are disgusting and I hope your dick rots."

The door opens and one of their people comes in, saying, "I brought the food sir and the guard suggested painkillers?"

Pelos nods, "Yes. Put it on the table and leave."

I watch as they set the tray on the nightstand and retreat from the room as though afraid they will be beaten. I catch Pelos staring at my legs and glare at him as I pick up the glass of water and two pills. They look like plain painkillers, and the servant said the guard suggested them. They are probably the safest thing in this house. I toss them to the back of my mouth and drink some water to wash them down.

As I drink, I feel Pelos touching my leg. I smack his hand away. "Touch me again and I'll rip it off and beat you with it."

He laughs at me, saying, "It's me or my father. You will be married to me and one of us will be fucking you till you're pregnant."

His words are horrifying and spark another train of thought, could I already be pregnant? I wasn't concerned with anything when Knox and I... oh boy. I need a calendar. But wait, can vampires even get women pregnant? Is that possible? Oh, no. Knox. What is he going to do when he finds me? He already seemed really possessive, and he didn't want me to leave on my own. I can't imagine what he is going to be like over this.

"You need to let me out of here. It's the only way you are going to survive. When the king gets here..."

Pelos laughs, "The king isn't coming to rescue you! You aren't worth that much to him. The only reason you are worth anything to us is because we can use you to join the properties and give us a larger holding." He stands and walks to the door, saying, "Besides, you have already been declared legally mentally incompetent." My jaw drops and he continues on, "Oh, you didn't know? Mommy had you declared mentally unstable and your inheritance stripped. Now you have nothing. No power of any kind and you are promised in marriage to me. As you are mentally unstable, your mother's agreement is enough for you to be considered married to me. If you cannot produce an heir, then I guess we will give you to the guards."

He closes the door, and I hear it lock. What if Knox doesn't come for me?

Knox

The scent has become clouded with the other scents of the day, and I don't know which way to go. My guards have caught up to me where I sit stopped at a crossroads, and the one on a bike takes off his helmet, asking, "Where next, sire?"

"I don't know, the scent is covered by everyone else." Oh goddess, what if they kill her? What if she is dying right now? I can't think about that. Wait, I know where to go. "I have it. If they aren't where I think they are, we'll need to search the city. For now, follow me."

Ingemar's house is nothing especially impressive, just another noble trying to impress other nobles. I sniff the air here as I get off my bike. The air still carries her scent, if she isn't here now, she was here recently. I look back at my guards, saying, "We are going into this house. And we are searching it, top to bottom. Three of you hold the exits, make noise if someone tries to leave. The rest of us will join you." My men nod and fall in behind me, other than the two that are circling the house to find the other exits, the third will be stationed outside the front door. "I feel certain she is in here. If we need to take down doors, we do so with care, as she may be behind the door."

At the front of the house, I pound on the door, listening to the sound as it travels through the house. A person of the house slings the door open, their mouth wide open to yell until they see me and choke, "St- *cough* sire! *cough* How, how can I help you?"

I push the person off to the side, telling them, "You can start by getting out of the way. And then go tell your employer that I am searching his house on suspicion of kidnapping." Their eyes bug out and they take off at a run.

We start with the first floor and though I can smell she passed through here, I know she isn't on this floor. She is in this house. On the second floor, we find a maid with roughly the same shape as Valdís tied up on a bed, naked. I have one of my men untie her and once the gag is removed I ask, "Are you ok?"

She is stuffing herself into her clothing as she says, "I will be fine now. I don't need this job. Don't need any job this bad! I am so out of here." I look to the guard that untied her and tell him, "Go ahead and escort her to the door so she can leave with my blessing."

He nods and the rest of us leave the room, finishing up the second floor with no other incidents. We go up to the third floor and I can smell her. I look both ways and I see Ingemar and his boy at one end of the hall, well; I guess now we know where she is.

Ingemar draws up all his courage as I get near so he can tell me, "Get out! You have no business here! This is a private home! Everyone will hear of your disregard for our laws!"

Clucking my tongue and shaking my head, I stop a step away from Ingemar. I can smell the stink of fear on him and his boy. "Ingemar, you didn't read any of the laws, did you?"

"Of course I did! That's how I know you can't just barge into my home!"

"Oh, but you did not. Or you would know that nobility holding technically belongs to the kings. They are on loan to you. And, anyone accused of a crime gives up the right to privacy until they are proven innocent, at which time they will receive reparation. You and your son are accused of kidnapping."

"We did no such thing! We collected my son's bride today, but that is hardly kidnapping."

"Ah, so you admit to collecting her. In front of witnesses, excellent." I hear Valdís try to shout my name in the room behind these two idiots and a scuffle as someone tries to silence her.

My eyes narrow as Ingemar tries once again to order me from his home. I reach up and tap his temple, and he goes down like a sack of potatoes. One of my guards snatches the boy off to the side as I step over the father. I try the door, and find it is locked. When I turn the knob anyway, I find out it is barred as well. I yell through the door, "Valdís, get away from the door!"

I study the door and find the two points where the bar is likely connected. A quick, light hit and they release from the walls and the door falls into the room.

Seventeen

V aldís

***

I am still sitting on the bed, trying to make sense of everything, when two guards run in and slam the door behind them. They grab a heavy bar and drop it into place, blocking the door in this strange room. As one they turn and look at me, my heart stops as they reach for me. I don't bother with screaming, because who is going to care here?

They snatch me up off the bed and hold me in front of them as they back into the corner farther from the door. Not that it is terribly far from the door, nothing is in this room. Since they are just holding me in place, I save my energy, what little I have. Listening intently, I try to figure out what they are running — oh. Knox must be here. Oh please, sweet Goddess, let him really be here! And come up to this floor. He must be. That's why they barred the door. Do they really think that is going to keep him out?

I hear Ingemar speaking, and the guards' grip me tighter. The fools didn't cover my mouth. I listen hard for the one voice I love more than any other. There! The guards begin to shake and I know I heard right. I've only got one chance to make sure he hears me, so I take a slow, deep breath and yell, "Knox!"

One guard hits me in the mouth and I taste blood as I struggle to free myself. The other hits me in the stomach, leaving me gasping for air. My ears are ringing, but I think I hear Knox saying something about the door. I hear a crash and the guards freeze even as I continue to struggle.

I look up in time to see Knox roar and then the guards hit the other wall as Knox takes me in his arms, "Are you ok? They hurt you? They. Hurt. You." I can hear the growl in his voice, I know he must smell the blood.

The guards were only doing as they were told, they have been hurt enough so I clutch Knox's shirt and say, "Please don't." Breathing still isn't the most comfortable thing, so I have to try again, "Please don't hurt them, it wasn't the guard's fault. Just get me out of here, please. Take me away from these people."

He lifts me into his arms so gently I could cry for it, though I won't. I tuck my head into his chest as he walks, I don't want to see any of them.

. . .

Outside, he takes me to a bike and sets me down next to it. "Can you, do you feel well enough to ride on a bike? We can take the car if you don't."

"I would ride on the back of a slug if it got me away from here," I tell him as I swing my leg over the bike so I can sit on the back.

He grins and climbs on, "Good." The guards are trailing out and he tells them, "We'll see you at the castle." One of them nods, and he starts the bike. I put my feet up on the pegs and he takes off. The trip to the castle is a lot faster when you take a vehicle the whole way. I should probably learn how to drive.

We arrive, and Epaphras runs out, he must have been waiting by the door. "I am so glad you are back safe," he studies me and says, "well, somewhat safe. Sire, I got everything readied as you had instructed before the incident. The holes are being repaired as we speak, and special presents are being added to the castle walls. All of them."

"Good. I will show her to her new room. The guards are following behind. They did very well today, have cook make a feast for them, and let the mead flow."

Epaphras nods and Knox sweeps me up into his arms again, carrying me into the castle. "You don't actually have to carry me. I could walk."

"I am well aware that you could walk. I want to carry you. Is that a problem?"

Only for my heart. "No, it's fine. Carry away, sire."

He chuckles, "I like it when you call me sire. Maybe you can call me that while I spank you sometime after you are feeling better."

His words make my pussy quiver, and I say, "Maybe we could try that after I have a shower?"

He stops before a door in the king's wing and sets me down. "This room hasn't let us enter for years. You'll have to try the door."

"What do you mean it hasn't let you enter? Rooms don't decide," I turn the knob and push the door open, "who gets to enter them. Whoa." The room is magnificent. "I don't belong in this room." When I turn back to him, I say, "This is too much. I can't stay in here. I'm not royalty."

He smiles at me, "If you didn't belong in here, the door wouldn't have opened for you," his hands go to my shoulders, turning me and gently pushing me over the threshold.

He pushes me until I am fully in the room, and he closes the door behind us. The room is red, black, and gold with white accents. There is so much scroll work throughout the room, I love it. A full wall is covered in bookshelves and there is a ladder. On wheels! The shelves have some books, but they are not full. If I get to stay here, I can add to the shelves... Stop that Valdís.

The bed is enormous, I didn't know they made them that big. "This room is, it's beautiful. And that bed, holy shit. I have never seen one so big." He mumbles something behind me and I turn to him, "What was that?"

He shrugs and says, "It was originally meant to hold thirteen."

"Wait, what? Thirteen? Thirteen people? Why?"

He guides me over to a small table and pulls out a chair, gesturing for me to sit. I do, and he seats himself in the chair next to me, saying, "There were originally twelve kings and we always thought there would still be twelve kings alive when she came into our lives."

"She? She who? Me? Can you explain maybe the entire story, instead of the specific reason for the size of the bed? I think I didn't ask the right question."

"I would like to wait to tell you the entire story. At least until Malic is home, and he has met you. If you can trust me that far?"

I look around me, "This room, this room is part of your explanation, isn't it? It goes back to what you said about the room accepting me. Okay. I think, since you have saved my life a couple times already that I can trust you for a little while longer." I look over at the bed again, "For now, I want a shower and then... Maybe we could try out the bed?"

He grins, saying, "We could try out the shower first if you like."

"Is the shower huge, too? Show me!"

He leads me to a door on the far side of the room and opens it, revealing an enormous bathroom. The shower at one end is enormous. There is another door that leads to a toilet, which I suddenly need. "Would you turn on the water while I use the facilities?"

He nods and heads for the glass doors of the shower while I head for the wooden door leading to the toilet. I emerge a few minutes later feeling ever so much better and Knox is in the shower covering all of his glorious body in soap.

I drop my clothing in record time and step into the shower, pressing my body against his back, my hands running up his chest, feeling those muscles. He turns in my arms and I let my hands explore his back.

"Let me wash you."

"You want to run your hands all over my body with soap? Yes, please."

Eirene

I sent the summons to Ingemar an hour ago, the dumb shit should have been here already. It's fine though. I will add it to the list of things I am going to tell him off about. How dare he kidnap her and manage to botch the whole deal? Now there is no way King Knox will let me have custody of her.

How am I going to spin this? I need everyone to believe that my daughter has been snatched away from me and that only my quick thinking has enabled me to save our homestead.

I am still pacing and trying to figure out how to spin this when Flavi taps on the door and escorts Ingemar in. He is sporting a lovely bruise on his temple, I hope his head is pounding. I wait for Flavi to leave before pointing at a chair and telling him, "Sit, you miserable fuck."

I watch him think about defying me and decide against it for whatever reason. He seats himself and I move to my desk, shoving my chair out of the way I stand so I can look down at this moron. "I would ask what you were thinking, but obviously you weren't. I will never understand just how a person could see a plan fail and then decide, I need to do the same fucking thing and surely it will work better this time? And I definitely won't ask how it is that you thought taking her to YOUR HOUSE! Your fucking house! I won't ask how you thought that was a good plan or if it occurred to you even once, you mangy scrap of old fur, that they might look for her there?"

He has leaned forward as I spoke and put his head to resting on his hands with his elbows on his knees. He is the picture of regret and I don't buy it for a minute. "Do you have anything to say for yourself?"

He looks up at me, saying, "I learned that the king is in love with her."

"Well, no shit. You are quick on the uptake. I never would have guessed that except for the reports from my spies, who are telling me exactly the same things yours tell you! How have you made it through life lacking simple observation skills? Now, I need you to listen, and I advise you to listen good. This is all so much bigger than just your stupid desire for a crown. I need to get my daughter away from the king, and you are still going to help me. All of your decision making privileges are revoked. If you are thinking about scratching your ass in public, you better clear it with me first! Do you understand?"

Of course he thinks he is going to have a spine now, "I will not! You will not run my life nor my decisions about how best to—" He is cut off as thunder rolls inside my office and looks at me with terror in his eyes, "What are you?"

"I am merely a representative for someone much more powerful than anyone on this island. I am acting on their orders and if you want to continue on living, I suggest you do as I say. They are very unhappy with you and it is only at my request that you are still alive. Don't make me rescind the request."

Eyes still wild, he nods, "I didn't realize."

"And that is why I was chosen. Most of you arrogant penis holders don't see me as a threat. It keeps things quiet and unnoticed until we choose to have things noticed. Which is why your decision making is cut off. You can't handle the responsibility of it and you make foolish choices. Now, you will go home and wait to see what the king decides to do about you. Since you were so cocky as to think no one would guess the people that were trying to marry into the family would take her, you are going to pay a price for your idiocy. Go! I am sick of looking at you!"

I watch him jump up and try not to run out the door. His movements are jerky and the door shuts quickly behind him. A voice sounds in my office, "You know I am not at my full power here, yet."

"I know. But he doesn't know that. And you are stronger every day as she weakens."

"I am. But what will you do if he becomes problematic?"

My lips curve in a smile as I answer, "Kill him, of course. As a sacrifice if I can arrange it. If not, then dead is still dead."

Laughter rolls through the room and he says, "Indeed. I think it is time for another sacrifice. Someone strong, make it last."

A shiver of anticipation rolls through me as I say, "Your will be done. I will find someone tonight."

Eighteen

Valdís

* * *

Rolling over in this giant bed, I look at Knox's beautiful form laying beside me. "What's next?"

He slants a look at me, "Next is you meet Malic. He is... a little more cranky than I am. And he isn't likely to be especially happy to see you. Though I can't say for sure. My brothers and I haven't been occupying the castle at the same time much in the last hundred or so years."

Tracing his muscles with a finger, I ask, "Why is that? Do you all not like each other anymore?"

"No, that isn't it at all." His breath catches as my tracing finger dips lower, "We, uh," he grabs my hand and holds it, "we are all just dealing with this immortal life as best we can. Since our brothers died, we have been reluctant to be gathered together. I don't know if that is a safety issue or perhaps a grief thing. We just haven't. Malic, he was always the biggest and strongest of us. He took the deaths of our brothers harder, I think, because he always took our protection as his job."

"Oh. That must have been really rough on him, to lose so many of you and feel like it was his fault."

"I think that may be the biggest part of it. He has always been very serious about anything he considers his responsibility. I don't know how he will feel about you coming into our lives right now. He may be... less than enthusiastic."

"Are you telling me in a very nice way that he might be angry about me being here?"

"That is a way of looking at it."

"Is he going to kill me?"

"Not while I live, no. I won't let him."

"So killing me is an option."

"Hm, I don't think he would literally kill you. Probably. Maybe by accident? Probably better if you don't seek him out right after he gets home. Possibly try to avoid him for a while."

"Well, I guess better that he kills me than I be forced to marry Pelos."

The arm curled around me tightens, "That is not an option. Period. Ingemar will face consequences for what he did, I just haven't decided what they will be. Which reminds me, I have some things I need to handle. Why don't you get some rest and we can have dinner together later?"

"Hm, yes. I like that idea. Somehow, being knocked out

is not as restful as one would think. What time is it, anyway?"

"It is nearly morning. The sun will be up soon. Get some rest, I'll have Epaphras bring you food in a few hours. Make sure you take your guards with you if you step foot outside this room. That includes the small courtyard attached. It doesn't matter that it is walled, you have someone with you if you step outside."

"Yes, sire," I say with a giggle.

He pulls me on top of him, saying, "Keep talking like that and I'll make you beg for mercy again."

A frisson of pleasure runs through my body at the thought, "Oh no, don't spank my big, round ass again. Anything but that."

He smacks my ass and rolls us so he is on top, saying, "Bad girl! I will be spanking you later."

* * *

* * *

Author's note

* * *

I hope you have enjoyed this start to my Vampire Kings series. I have three other series to tide you over till book two comes out, you can find samples and an offer for a free book in the back of the book. For now, let's dive into the beginning of book two, Shame of a Vampire King.

Nineteen

Malic

* * *

Epaphras has already warned me there is a woman in the castle that I will need to deal with. What is Knox thinking? Why would he have one of those crown seeking twats hanging about in the castle? This is what comes from all that fucking of the humans he does. My brothers all think that I do not know what they do while they are out roaming the world, but they would be wrong. I know where they are and who they are with at all times. Just because we need our time apart does not mean my job as a protector is over.

My failure to protect them did not absolve me from the job, and being apart certainly won't do it. Epaphras' warning convinced me to return early without telling anyone. I want to surprise everyone with my return, most especially this Valdís. However, since no one is expecting me, I do have to dock the boat alone. No great hardship, just a little more focus.

Once I have my ship moored, I head directly for the garage nearby. There is a strange scent in the garage, faint but still present. It is the best thing I have ever smelled. What is that? Shrugging it off, I get on one of the bikes. I hate trying to squeeze myself into the cars. They are built for smaller people than I. Roaring off through the tunnels; I wonder just what state will the castle be in?

Knox has always been the most kind of us all. And the most soft-hearted. One good sob story and he would give her half the castle. I was soft once, and it cost me my brothers. It won't happen again. That smell is there again as I get to the other end of the tunnel. It is much stronger here, more distracting. Focus Malic, no distractions.

My appearance surprises the guards as I step off the elevator. They were in defensive positions though, so I smile at them, saying, "Excellent work. Did you notify anyone that I am here?"

"Yes, we followed protocol. I need to inform that you are not a threat before half of the guard is dispatched this way."

"Go ahead, but have them keep it quiet that I am here. I want to surprise my brother."

"As you wish, sire."

He turns and speaks into his comm device while I tell the other guard, "Report. What has happened recently? Why is there a woman in the castle?"

The guard tells me how this woman arrived at the castle

one day wanting to petition. Ever since she arrived, people from outside the castle have been trying to kill or kidnap her and the castle itself has suffered two explosions. He also informs me of the additional security measures installed on the outer walls and the recent kidnapping.

"Thank you. Do you smell that?" I can smell that scent on the breeze. It is the best scent I have ever smelled. My instincts want me to follow that scent to its source and devour it. I won't, but I will find out where it comes from. After I see my brother.

The guard looks at me like I have grown a second head as he tells me, "No, sire. I only smell the regular smells. Perhaps the castle smells different because you have been away so long?"

"Yes, that must be it. Thank you." I leave him and head into the castle, where the scent is so much stronger. Maybe it is just the way the castle smells now?

As I stride through the halls, Epaphras stops and stares at me from a crossing of halls, "Sire, you weren't due for days yet! Your room isn't ready. Why would you not give me a warning? Oh! You kings just do as you please, no regard for us working folk!"

I laugh, "I'm sorry Epaphras. I wanted to surprise my brother and catch him before he leaves."

"Well, your room isn't ready yet. It won't be until tonight. The only room currently ready is the guest room that was so recently blown up and repaired. And your brother isn't planning to leave anytime soon. I could have told you that if you had let me know you were coming early."

Not leaving? "What do you mean, my brother isn't leaving?"

"Exactly what I said. He is staying, he has been waiting for your arrival. Did you injure your brain on the way in?"

The scent gets stronger and I close my eyes briefly, "Do you smell that Epaphras?"

"Smell what? What is it with you all and the smells lately? Are you sick? Can you lot get sick?"

"I'm not the only one that smells something?"

He scowls at me, saying, "No, your brother and Valdís both smell something lately that I can't seem to detect. I think you are all nuts. If you don't need anything, *sire*, I will be off to have your room aired and cleaned."

I can't help but laugh as he stomps off. I call after him, "Where is my brother?"

"In his office!"

Shaking my head, I turn the opposite direction he is heading and start for my brother's office. I don't bother with knocking when I get to the door, I just open it and step in. He looks up from the paperwork he is handling, and for just a fleeting second, I swear I saw fear in his eyes. What would he have to fear from me? Unless the fear isn't for himself, but the little twat living somewhere in the castle. "Hello brother. Tell me what has been happening in my absence."

He sighs, saying, "I suppose you do need to hear it all."

I sit opposite him, saying, "Before you start, what is the scent that is throughout the castle?"

"Smells like everything good in the world? Like you might die if you can't find it?" His description is so accurate I am a little afraid, but I nod and he says, "That is Valdís."

"You could just tell me what it is, absolutely ridiculous to attribute something that smells that good to a bitch that is here to use us."

Knox growls at me. Of all the shit, the motherfucker growled at me before he says, "Malic, I need you to hold your tongue until you meet her or I am going to rip it out again."

He is so serious, what has this bitch done to him? While I am not afraid of Knox, I humor him, saying, "Fine. I will withhold judgement for now."

Knox tells me about the things that have been going on since the day that this Valdís appeared at the door seeking the right to petition. His telling of the tale is more thorough than the guard. Her mother is seeking to strip her of her inheritance? Her father's best friend wants to force her to marry his son and went so far as to kidnap her? What the fuck? Why? I know the holding the family has, it is nice but nothing that special.

"Knox, why? What is so special about her that these people that should care for her are trying to eliminate her as threat one way or another?"

Knox looks away, toward our wing of the castle, saying, "The room accepted her Malic."

He could have ripped my tongue out and it would have hurt less. "Don't fuck with me Knox, there is no way she has appeared after all this time. Not after we all finally gave up."

"I didn't want to believe it either, brother. There were

other signs, the scent of her, for one. Then she was kidnapped by Ingemar's people and I couldn't focus. Finding her took hours longer than it should have, solely because I was too distraught to see the obvious culprits. Once I did, we recovered her quickly. I haven't quite decided what his punishment will be, perhaps you would like to help make the decision?"

"Well, that is appealing. I think I will take you up on that. But first, I want to question her."

His eyes narrow as he tells me, "Maybe meet her and set up a time for questions later? Keeping in mind that she is not on trial."

"I will try. Let's get this over with."

He sends for Epaphras, who likely knows where everyone in the castle is, as he is one of my sets of eyes and ears, not that Knox knows that. Epaphras enters the room with a scowl, saying, "Yes, sire?"

Knox looks confused until I grin at him and he just shakes his head at me, asking, "Epaphras, do you know where Valdís is currently?"

"Yes. She has just gone back to her rooms a bit ago, as you arrived actually," he gives me a hard stare and I grin back unrepentant, "she had been in the kitchen eating and visiting with Cook."

Knox nods, "Yes, that's right. Cook is one of her family employees' cousin. He is the one that passed the letters from his cousin to us. I need to thank him for that. You say she is in her room again?"

"Yes. If there is nothing else you require of me, I am quite busy right now with unplanned room readying," he says as he glares at me. Snickering, I turn my face away. I hear him turn and exit the room, as the door clicks shut Knox bursts with laughter.

"I haven't seen him so mad in years! What did you do?"

Still grinning, I tell him, "I didn't let him know I would be home early. He is mad because my room isn't ready already."

Knox stands, shaking his head at me, "You can't be making the people that keep the castle running mad, we are all going to end up with something vile in our shoes. Come on, I'll take you to meet her."

I didn't really believe him when he said the room accepted her until he led me to our wing. Straight to the door I had begun to pray would never open. Directly to the concentration of the best scent I have ever smelled. Right toward the woman I can't accept.

He knocks on the door and I hear her say come in, the guards on either side of her door are ramrod straight, as though they can sense my mood. Knox opens the door and a wave of her scent hits me. The smell of her makes me weak. Which is exactly why I cannot have anything to do with her, I was weak once and my brothers paid for it.

I follow him, keeping my eyes on the floor until he stops and says, "Valdís, I want to introduce you to my brother, Malic."

I finally look at her, and I am lost, her olive skin and curves. That long dark hair. She stands from the chair she was sitting in and extends her hand, saying, "Hello, it's nice to meet you. My, you smell as good as Knox does. Are you guys bathing in something?" Knox laughs as I struggle to make my hand obey me, and reaching out, I take her hand and the contact hits us both. Raw energy surging between us as she clasps my rough hand with her soft one. Her eyes drift closed and her mouth forms an oh as the scent of her arousal fills the air.

I snatch my hand from hers, saying, "I will see you tomorrow. I have many questions for you about the current situation." With that, I turn and leave the room as fast as I can.

I hear her behind me asking Knox in a breathy voice, "What was that?"

As I shut the door behind me, he answers, "That was a man running from his destiny."

Author's Note

This is a completed series, and one of my favorites to have written. If you would like to keep up with what I am writing next, sign up for my newsletter at RhiannonFutch Writer.com. If early access is your favorite thing ever, you should visit my community where I am sharing the next series as I write it at Rhiannon's Ream Stories Community.

Rhiannon writes steamy paranormal romance. She is an avid reader of many authors in a variety of genre though she tends more toward paranormal.

She has three former pound puppies that she dotes on and three daughters that she adores.

Rhiannon has lived in multiple states though she is currently residing in North Carolina. Wandering, witching, and reading with her puppies and husband are what she does when she isn't writing.

To learn about what is happening in Rhiannon's world and get loads of pupper cuteness, sign up for the newsletter here.

Mercy of the Vampire King

Shame of the Vampire King

Pursuit of the Vampire King

Prey of the Vampire King

Reign of the Vampire King

Coming Soon

Love and Vampires Series

Olivia's Fall

Olivia's Prison

Olivia's Flight

Olivia's Family

Warriors of the Old Gods

A Dream of Blood

A Dream of Wolves

A Dream of Stone

A Dream of Ravens

A Dream of Bones